JALOK

CONQUERED WORLD: BOOK FOURTEEN

ELIN WYN

CLOCK
WALK
PUBLISHING

DOTTIE

I woke up with the rising sun as I had the day before. I'd spent the majority of the last two weeks in a windowless lab inputting data that, ultimately, made no sense to our computers.

It didn't make me any happier about being cooped up, but it was nice to be home for a bit. I worked out of Kaster, my family's home city.

When I first took this contract with General Rouhr and his scientists, they wanted me to move to Nyhiem to work.

I declined without thinking twice.

When bad things happened, they happened in Nyhiem first. The anti-alien radicals had a huge foothold in that city. Not long ago, there'd been a shooting that nearly killed the mayor of Nyhiem and her personal bodyguard or something like that.

No way was I about to relocate to such a dangerous place.

Besides, I loved Kaster. My family had lived there since the city was first founded. The Xathi did a number on it which was all the more reason or me not to leave.

We needed everyone to pitch in for the rebuilding efforts.

The sunlit stretch of the tent above me did nothing to stop the brightness of the morning sun from creeping in. That's how I liked it. I was a sunlight creature.

Cloudy days put me in a bad mood. Back home, the running joke was that I was secretly part plant and that's why I became an environmental scientist.

I stepped out of my tent to bask in the morning rays. I arrived here yesterday, too late in the evening to warrant setting up my equipment, and now I'd need to make up some time.

This was my first time back since the Puppet Master was attacked by a group of anti-alien radicals. While I was glad I wasn't here during the attack, I felt terrible for not being there to defend the Puppet Master.

Not that I'd really have been much help, but I should have been able to do something, anything, right?

His exposed vines had been singed and slashed. Today, I planned to take samples from the wounds to see what the radicals used.

A hole had been blown in the northeast side of the crater making a tunnel. I walked across the expanse of the crater and through the mouth of the tunnel.

This was obviously one of the main routes to the Puppet Master's home, as thick emerald vines lined the walls. The deeper into the earth I went, the fewer injuries I saw on the Puppet Master's vines.

When I found a location free of injuries, I placed my hand against a cool, firm vine.

"Welcome, Dottie," came the layered voice of the Puppet Master in my head. *"I predicted you'd arrive here soon."*

"How are you?" I asked. "Are you in any pain?"

"Some, but I will soon heal."

"How do you heal?" I took out my recorder. Since the Puppet Master's voice was purely telepathic, I couldn't record him directly. I planned on repeating everything he said to me out loud. It was clumsy, but it worked.

"I generate my own healing enzymes that can repair wounds," he explained. *"Don't be too impressed. You do the same thing when you're injured."*

I laughed as I repeated his answer.

"At the core of all things, I am a lifeform just as you are,

despite the fact that I am what you would call ancient," he continued. "Pay close enough attention and you will find we have more similarities than we do differences."

That's why I loved talking to the Puppet Master. He had the ability to make me feel so small yet so significant at the same time.

"We refer to you as male," I prompted. "Does that mean there are females too?"

"Male and female refers to reproductive capabilities. My species does not reproduce. We are eternal."

"Then where did you come from?"

"That even I can't tell you," he said. "One instant I was not. The next instant I was. In the history of this universe, I am but a youngling in the footsteps of those that came before me. While I may have knowledge over my eons of existence, I have but scratched the surface of our reality."

"You're a mystery." I affectionately patted the vines. "I like solving mysteries."

"I will tell you what I know, although I can't promise your limited brain will be able to comprehend it," he said.

"Hey!"

"That was not meant to be insulting. It is simply true."

"I know," I sighed.

"You're very intelligent for a human." A thin tendril reached out to wrap around my wrist. It was the Puppet Master's equivalent of a pat on the shoulder.

"You're lucky I like you so much," I teased. "Let's move back to your healing abilities. Do they extend to only your own body or the rest of the planet?"

"The rest of the planet is my body. I am simply the heart and the mind."

"I know but I need a way to measure that," I chuckled.

"Some things are incapable of being measured in a lab."

"Don't start getting philosophical on me."

"All life is philosophical when it contemplates its existence, child."

"Really? Then we have something else in common."

I liked explaining new things to the Puppet Master. It made me feel less useless, like I had my own information to share with this all-knowing, seemingly omnipotent entity.

"Long ago back on Earth a bunch of guys sat around and asked questions that appeared to have simple answers but were really far more complicated than originally anticipated. Even with all of our advancements, we still can't answer most of them."

"Such as?"

"My favorite has always been 'what is the true reality?' If a group of people simultaneously witness the same event, each has a slightly different perception. Which one is the true one?"

"Excellent," the Puppet Master hummed.

"What is?"

"The answer you seek is found in the question itself."

And that's how I learned the Puppet Master enjoyed philosophy.

JALOK

Toe to heel, Cazak and I crept up on our unwary prey. Looming, half rebuilt buildings hemmed us in on either side, making our task all the more dangerous.

The two of us were supposed to be on patrol, checking for any glaring structural issues and making sure the anti-alienists weren't lurking about Nyheim proper.

Ever since the unrest during the election and the attack on the Puppet Master, command was extra paranoid about even the slightest problem.

All three Strike teams found themselves utilized for even routine patrols such as this one.

"Do you see it?" Cazak spoke in a low tone, because

a whisper can carry much further in the dark than one would suspect.

I squinted, peering in the gloom, until I saw a flash of light behind a rubbish bin. A spindly leg splayed out as a deer-like creature rooted about for scraps.

"Yeah. It's a tiny one."

"Even small ones can be a threat, especially to a civilian."

Grunting, I drew my side arm. The sleek pistol had been painted unreflective black, making it perfect for urban stealth ops. It seems like overkill for such a tiny, delicate seeming creature.

Luurizi, however, could be known as vicious creatures that could easily kill a human. Or even a Valorni. The little shits would charge at damn near anything, and their feet were so sharp they could pierce all but the highest grade armor plating.

Even my innate sheath of scales wouldn't prove sufficient against its attack. I deployed them anyway, because sometimes the hollow rail gun rounds could ricochet after impact.

Cazak grinned, flexing his own scales into view but he still ducked behind the corner of a building for cover.

"Coward," I spoke in a low voice as I creep up for a better shot.

"Don't talk to me that way. Who was it who

recommended your transfer from the Ground Team to Strike Team Three? Show some gratitude."

"Yeah, thanks for getting me this sweet gig where I kill fairytale creatures in the most gruesome manner possible. In the dark. In the middle of the night—"

"Are you going to talk it to death?"

"You've been trying to do that to me for years."

The Luurizi's head popped up, focusing its gaze in our direction. Our voices had grown louder during the exchange, it seemed.

With a shrill cry akin to broken glass, it galloped across the pavement.

Srell.

"Now look at what you've done."

I didn't have time for a retort. The Luurizi loped ever faster, then drove its forelegs into the ground. Its back legs gathered together with the front, and then it bunched up its body and sprang, all in the matter of a split second.

My gaze tracked its flight, and I aimed my pistol for its midsection. One squeeze of the trigger, and the creature exploded in midair, showering me with bits of bone and gooey tissue.

"Double Srell." Wiping myself clean, I staggered back onto the main thoroughfare while Cazak laughed hysterically.

"Come on, hero. Patrol's over. Let's go grab some beverages."

Grumbling, I fell into step beside him. We headed toward the towering buildings of the city proper, where the damage had already been largely repaired.

"Things sure have been crazy lately."

I glanced over at Cazak, and noted his worried frown.

"Yes, it's been hectic for a while, and I don't see it calming down anytime soon."

"This is a strange place to be a Skotan. Cooperating with other races instead of dominating them."

The words bubbled out of my mouth before I could really consider them. "Do you ever think we'll find a way to get back home?"

"We're going to stop at the pub first, I told you—"

"No, I mean, the homeworld."

Cazak's jaw worked silently, and I could feel the longing from him as well. "I don't know. Maybe they can figure out a way to open a rift to get us home, someday."

"If we're allowed to use rifts again."

"True."

We walked in silence, our destination locked in for the recreational district. There we would find a pub friendly to us off-worlders, where you can be around other people who got it, even if they weren't Skotan.

Cazak and I ordered some drinks and sat down at a booth. I barely tasted my drink, and I doubt he enjoyed his own much more.

"I'd like to go home, someday."

Cazak looked over at me and shrugged as if it doesn't matter, though I knew it did. "What's the matter, don't like this place?"

"Well, it's not that. I'm certainly not a xenophobe like the anti-alienists. It's just that—on the homeworld, we belonged. Here, we'll never really fit in. Or at least, that's what it feels like."

"If you were back home, you would probably be on a ship fighting the Xathi."

"That's where I *want* to be." I took a long pull from the bottle, and set the half empty vessel down. "I belong in battle, fighting an enemy I can see, not having to worry about pissing off a giant space lettuce or having some invisible, non-corporeal being root around in my brain and make me a meat suit."

We headed out into the night. I'd thought Cazak was done with the conversation, but he surprised me. "The Xathi are terrifying, Jalok. Worse than any of that, if you ask me."

"Well, I didn't ask you, did I? Fighting is what I do. Soldiering is what I was made for. Cooling my heels on this planet while our brothers and sisters die fighting those damn bugs is torture."

"Look at it this way." Cazak spread his hands out, as if encompassing the galaxy between them. "They're at home, fighting for the good of Skotans everywhere, and we're here, fighting for the good of Skotans—and humans and K'ver and all the rest. You can't be everywhere at once. But you can make a difference right here."

"Yeah, but we're not supposed to be here. That's all I'm saying. Everything is wrong about this planet. The others might love it, but Skotan are supposed to spend most of our time in high gravity."

"Yes, but that makes us stronger here, and gives us greater mass."

"That's true, but our hearts evolved to beat against a much stronger G-force. I was reading a briefing from the science office about concerns that our hearts might beat too quickly and lead to a risk of cardiovascular disease."

Cazak snorted, and flashed an uncaring glare my way. "You think too much. Look at you, you're a freaking walking tank and you want to read science reports? You should be balancing a sweet scaly thing on each one of those massive guns when you hit the sack tonight. Instead you want to act like a galaxy class nebbish."

"I find science interesting," I scowled. "What else am I supposed to do to pass the time during my days off?"

"Drinking and screwing, you ignoramus. You're with Strike Team Three now. We're the best of the best of the best!" He slapped me hard on my shoulder, and I let the matter drop.

We trudged on for a time without speaking. At length Cazak glanced over and punched me on the arm.

"Hey, if you want to feel less homesick, we could practice the traditional songs."

"Have you heard yourself? Besides, Skotan ballads were meant to be sung on the Skotan homeworld. They just don't sound the same any place else."

That ended the debate, for now.

All I knew at the time was, while many of our new allies were good people, I just wanted to go back where I belonged.

DOTTIE

"We have a big day ahead of us today," I announced as I settled into a comfortable sitting position inside the tunnel.

"You say that every time," the Puppet Master replied telepathically.

"Because it's true every time," I countered. "Almost every experiment we run is groundbreaking, simply because my people have never even imagined something like you."

And that excitement was part of what pulled me out of camp every morning, hurrying down into the tunnels.

Who could resist being a part of making scientific history?

Sitting on the dirt with my back against one of the

Puppet Master's vines, I started setting up my equipment. I carefully attached tiny neuro-monitors to the flesh of the vine.

"Did that hurt?"

"Did what hurt?" The Puppet Master replied.

"Never mind."

My equipment was acceptable, but it wasn't top of the line. I only got the top of the line stuff if I checked it out from the Nyhiem lab.

I knew that some of the aliens traveled through what seemed like essentially portals, but that method of travel wasn't available to the average scientist yet.

If I wanted to go to Nyhiem, I'd have to go the old-fashioned way and wait for a ride on a shuttle.

That wasn't something I really wanted to do. It'd cut into my time with the Puppet Master.

So I just hadn't bothered to go.

"A wise choice," the Puppet Master whispered to my consciousness.

"You can read my thoughts even if I'm not attempting to directly commune with you?"

"You've made physical contact." A tendril tapped me on the shoulder and pointed to the vine I leaned up against. *"Once direct contact is made, a link between our minds is forged forever. As long as you are in my vicinity, I'm listening and can reply."*

"Is that how you commune with the living trees?" I asked.

"No," he sighed. *"They don't possess enough sentience to forge a stable connection."*

"Then how did you direct them before?" No one had ever come up with a viable theory for that, and we still speculated wildly back at the lab.

What can I say? Scientists are as easily amused as anyone else.

"I," the Puppet Master started to explain, then halted. *"I do not know how to answer that. It is similar to if I asked you how you breathe or how you think. I perform the action without conscious effort."*

"Interesting." I tapped my chin with a stylus. "I have an idea."

"What's that?"

"We're going to do a different kind of experiment."

I pushed myself up from the ground and brushed the dirt off the seat of my pants.

Motioning for the Puppet Master to follow me, in whatever way he was capable of doing so, I walked out of the tunnel. The earth around my feet shifted as I walked as the Puppet Master's vines extended out.

I climbed out of the crater.

Halfway up, I lost my footing. It wasn't a far fall but the Puppet Master burrowed up vines to catch me anyway.

"Thanks," I gave the vine a pat.

Once out of the crater, I headed to a copse of trees deeper into the forest. Since the Xathi invasion, the creature populations dropped considerably.

Walking through the forest was a death wish before. Now, it was just highly unrecommended.

Which didn't seem like a bad idea to most people, but I knew it was a sign that our ecosystem had been badly disrupted.

I stopped in a small clearing. Thanks to the Puppet Master and the efforts of dedicated citizens, the forest had begun to grow back.

It wasn't what it used to be. I could still see chunks of sky through the canopy and most of the trees still had tinges of brown death on their trunks.

It was progress, though. The forest would be in top shape in no time.

The Puppet Master's vines rose out of the earth beside me. I reached out and pressed my palm against one.

"It's my duty to advise you that being here is unwise," the Puppet Master warned. *"The creatures of the forest have begun to return to this area."*

"Why? I have the ultimate protection." I gave the vines another pat.

"What sort of experiment are you trying to perform?"

"I'm going to attract one of the sentient trees. You're

going to stop it from attacking me. While you do that, you're going to tell me everything you're thinking and feeling."

"Thinking is an inaccurate term for what I do."

"I know but I'm human, remember? Limited understanding of beings and brains bigger than my own. Now, will you do this?"

The Puppet Master went silent for a few moments. *"A Durindium is already on your scent,"* he stated.

"A what?"

That was far faster than I expected, and I jumped to switch gears from the theoretical to the very, very immediate.

Before the Puppet Master could respond, a creature leaped down from the canopy above.

Its body was long, lean, and feline in proportions. Sharp obsidian talons dug into the earth as it landed. Its face looked avian with a sharp, bony beak. Around its neck was a fan of growths that looked like thick flower petals.

It reminded me of a lion's mane in the old vids from Earth.

It eyed me with its split pupil stare and let out a shriek that made my ears ring.

"Find a way to stop it from attacking me." My voice shook as I spoke. "And let me know how you're doing it."

Whose idea was this?

"Its willpower is substantial," the Puppet Master replied.

The Durindium slowly circled me.

I pivoted, keeping my body square with its body. It was looking for a weak point, a good place to pounce.

"Is willpower a key factor in determining how you control another creature?" I kept my voice steady.

Focusing on the experiment would help keep my fear under control. I had a feeling the Durindium could smell fear.

"Yes. Right now, I'm negotiating with the Durindium's essence, it's soul if you will," he explained.

The Durindium snapped it's beak and hissed.

"It doesn't look like it's going well."

"It's not."

"Why would you tell me that," I whimpered.

"Did you not wish to know?"

The Durindium swiveled to face me head on. It lowered its haunches in preparation to spring forward right at me.

"Now would be a good time to wrap up negotiations," I pleaded.

The Puppet Master didn't answer.

A wave of doubt washed over me. What if the Puppet Master wasn't my friend at all? What if he was still an enemy of the humans at heart?

The Durindium leaped forward. I closed my eyes and curled myself downward as if that would protect me from its slashing talons.

I heard its feet land on the forest floor but no impact came. Its hot breath whipped through my hair.

Against my better judgment, I peeked up.

I was face to face with the Durindium, my nose less than an inch from its protruding beak.

I raised a shaking hand and touched the Puppet Master's vines, curling around my feet.

"So," I gulped. "The negotiations went well?"

"I convinced the creature that eating you will bring on my wrath," the Puppet Master supplied.

Guilt hit me. I shouldn't have doubted him.

Slowly my stomach began to unknot.

"Can you walk me through your process? I was too busy being terrified the first time."

"Certainly."

The Puppet Master must've done something else to the Durindium because it suddenly let out a yelp and darted back into the forest.

I released the breath I didn't realize I'd been holding.

At the Puppet Master's insistence, I agreed to go back to the safety of the crater. Once I was seated with my equipment once more, the Puppet Master began his explanation.

"*What occurs between myself and another lifeform cannot be accurately put into your human vernacular,*" he started. "*However, I'll do my best. My lifeforce pulses through this planet like a network of rivers. All lifeforms on this planet drink from my rivers. Parts of me are parts of them. Do you understand?*"

"Partially." I recorded a few notes in my field datapad and nodded for the Puppet Master to keep going.

"*I control my lifeforce, even the parts that are in other lifeforms. My lifeforce becomes their lifeforce. When I take control of another creature, I'm simply taking control of my own life force.*"

"Why was it harder to control the Durindium than it is to control the sentient trees?" I asked.

"*The Durindium is an active hunter, a strategist. Its intelligence is greater than that of the sentient trees. It's clever enough to detect an outside force in its mind and fight against it. The one that attacked you was also desperate. Its natural prey populations are far too small.*"

"I understand." I took down more notes. "Could you've used vines to directly manipulate the Durindium?"

"*If I'd planted one of my seeds within the Durindium, I could have. However, it's more likely that would've killed it. The sentient trees make excellent hosts since they are closer to plants than animals. They are infinitely simpler than creatures like the Durindium, who are more like animals than plants."*

"Is that why you can't control humans or aliens?"

"I never said I can't control them."

Wait. What?

"If I were to try, it would take a great deal of energy and it would be a lengthy battle for control. You humans and your alien friends have my lifeforce within you. You take it in every time you eat a plant or an animal from the forest."

"I appreciate that you've never tried to take over my brain," I chuckled.

"Brain is inaccurate," the Puppet Master corrected. *"But since I can't draw a more apt parallel, you're welcome for not taking over your brain."*

With a laugh, I checked the neuro-monitors I had hooked up earlier. The monitors recorded great spikes of energy during the time of my ill-planned experiment.

My field equipment couldn't fully analyze the spikes so I send them over to my lab back in Kaster.

If I couldn't complete a satisfactory analysis there, I'd have to send it to the lab in Nyhiem.

"If a creature came from somewhere else, but took in your life force, would you be able to exert control over it?" I asked.

"Yes, with one exception."

That didn't sound good. Not at all.

"Which is?"

"My race doesn't have a proper name for them. Millennia ago, when there were more of us and we were able to communicate, we called them the Ancient Enemies. They were older than us, more powerful than us, and capable of siphoning out lifeforce until there was nothing left."

"How awful." I made note of this new, unsettling information. "What else can you tell me about them?"

"Nothing." The Puppet Master sounded mournful. *"That's all I know. My race never learned how to combat them. We never discovered where they were from or what their purpose was, other than stealing our lives."*

"Is that something we should be worried about?"

"They haven't been active for thousands of years. I suspect they've moved on to a more plentiful galaxy."

I entered this new information into my notes.

Somehow, the Puppet Master's words didn't bring me any comfort.

JALOK

Hunched over, elbows on knees, the turbulence jostled me about to the limits the shuttle's crash webbing would allow. Air travel has never caused me much problem, but I had to feel for Navat.

The big Valorni sat a few seats to my right, and struggled immensely to keep down his last meal.

Our team leader, Sk'lar stood in the aisle between us grunts, not bothered in the least by the turbulence. As a highly modified K'ver, his ebony skin was laced with circuitry, connecting a series of implants that let him accomplish feats like remaining upright inside an airship shaking like a leaf in the wind.

"Kaster's central city square has become the site of a massive protest by the anti-alien movement." His black eyes constantly scanned the faces of our team, making sure we were still paying attention, despite the turbulence. "Likewise, counter protesters have swollen the city block far past capacity. In short, it's hot, cramped, miserable and there are thousands of angry people."

"Sounds like a hot date night with your woman," Cazak quipped. Some chuckles went around the cabin despite Sk'lar's withering glare.

"Knock it off." Sk'lar's voice dropped an octave, and he gave Cazak a particularly stern glare. "Our job here is to quell any violence, period. If we can't be professional amongst ourselves, how are we going to keep everyone else calm?"

"With all respect, boss." We turned our gazes on Tyehn, who had his hand sheepishly raised. "A little ribbing does not make us unprofessional."

"I don't recall exceptions about ribbing your commanding officer, soldier. If you don't have anything useful to contribute, shut your mouth and load up with non-lethal rounds."

"Non lethals?" Cazak's voice took on a whining quality. "When do we just get to bust heads like the old days?"

"You have your orders. We want this situation contained with a minimum of collateral damage. Once we touch down at Kaster, we will coordinate our efforts with civilian security. Does anyone have any questions?"

Tyehn and Cazak put their hands up.

"About the mission?"

They both lowered them back down.

"I've got a question."

Sk'lar glared at me, but nodded curtly, giving me permission to speak.

"If the humans hate our guts, how are we supposed to keep things calm? We're the ones being protested against. Shouldn't we at least be wearing the holo-disguises?"

"General Rouhr wants the anti-alienists to see that we're not the enemy. That we're just here to keep the peace." He shrugged. "Apparently some of them heard rumors we can shapeshift or something, which isn't helping with the whole trust issue."

He scanned the cabin, then nodded as if to himself.

"Good. Now, Strike Team Three has a reputation with command for being a bunch of, to use a human term, 'cowboys.' I'd like to change that perception. Clear?"

"Yes, sir." We all said raggedly. Sk'lar sat down to make adjustments to his own munitions.

"He was more mellow before he started screwing around with Phryne," muttered Cazak. "Isn't that supposed to work the other way around?"

Sk'lar glanced our way sharply, but didn't offer any rebuke.

The shuttle banked into a hard turn, throwing us against our crash webbing. Engines decreased their rhythmic throb as we slowed our pace and came in for a landing. There was a thump beneath our feet as the landing pylons deployed, then the ship settled in with surprising gentleness.

"All right, lock and load." Sk'lar lead the way down the gangplank as Team Three disembarked. As soon as the ramp dropped down, we could already hear the cacophony of shouting from the town square.

Everywhere we looked, there was a press of sapient beings.

Civilian security had erected waist high barriers, keeping the protesters and counter protesters roughly divided on either side of the square. However, the barriers were easily circumnavigated, and there was a near constant parade of traffic back and forth. As we watched a group of masked anti-alienists leaped across the barrier and charged across the short stretch of flagstone separating them from the other side.

They heaved metal canisters over the barriers, then ran back where they came from. We couldn't see where the canisters hit, but several clouds of noxious smoke indicated where they had fallen.

"Look alive, people. Navat, you and I will seek out

the officers in charge of security here. We'll use comms to coordinate. Tyehn, we can assume that the anti-alienists are the more likely to be violent, so keep watch on their side. Let me know the second another group tries to cross those barriers."

He turned his black eyes upon myself and Cazak.

"You two. Those masked men. I want their asses."

So much for keeping the peace. But honestly, it didn't look like we had much choice.

"Yes, sir." Cazak headed off at a dead run, an eager gleam in his eyes. As I hastened to follow, Sk'lar bellowed after us.

"Alive. Take them alive."

The sight of two heavily armed Skotan soldiers beating feet cleared a path before us. Protesters on both sides gaped at our surprising speed. My scales rippled out along my body as I prepared for combat.

Cazak reached the barrier first. He leaped into the air, drew his legs up under his body, and cleared the barrier by a good three feet. On his way down he lashed out with both feet into the sternum of an anti-alien protester.

I didn't know if the man was threatening Cazak in any way, but I did know that he wouldn't be causing anyone any trouble laying on his back gasping for breath.

The relatively lower gravity on our new planet

allowed us Skotan to perform feats which were out of reach to our allies. I bunched my legs up and leaped into the air over the barrier, but I cleared the barrier by nearly five feet, putting me high above the throng.

That viewpoint allowed me to spot the handful of masked men as they cut through the crowd like a wedge. They were even knocking down and trampling over their own allies.

"Nine o'clock, Cazak." I landed in a run and stretched my legs out for maximum speed. A protester, his face a mask of rage, swung an improvised club my way. I pointed my rifle and squeezed the trigger, sending a slow velocity latex based projectile into his sternum. The man's cheeks poofed out, his club clattered to the ground, and he crumpled into a heap.

Anyone else who even looked like they were going to be a problem got the same treatment.

The mercy rounds created a kind of silly sounding *floop* when fired. Judging by the *floops* which came from behind me, my team were likewise deploying their weaponry with a liberal hand.

Sure, those protesters would be hurting for days after the riot.

But I'm not the one who ruined a perfectly good day by protesting another sapient species' right to exist.

If it had been up to me, we'd all be at the nearby beach having a—what did the humans call it?—a Luau.

That sounded nice.

Instead, I found myself in a swirl of sweating, furious humanity who all wanted my blood and I was not allowed to kill any of them. The press of the crowd closed in behind me, swallowing Cazak.

I was not particularly worried about him, or the rest of the team. They could take care of themselves.

I was worried about myself, because at that point I was facing down dozens of protesters, some armed with bladed weapons. My thumb switched the rifle from single shot to free fire mode. I swung the rifle in an arc, and the barrel spewed a sadistic spread of non-lethal agony throughout the would be attackers.

People always think they could tough it out until they took a mercy round. Then even the biggest, baddest Valorni will crumple into a heap.

But the crowd was all around me, and multiple hands clamped onto my arms. My rifle was pulled out wide, useless at such close quarters, and blows rained down on my head and shoulders.

My scales absorbed the worst of it, but the sheer weight of their numbers threatened to overwhelm me. If I went down there, I would die, simple as that.

With a sudden surge, I threw off most of my attackers and leaped into the air, climbing upon a communications pylon some twenty feet above the grand melee.

I reached back and tossed off the fool still clinging to my neck.

Some of the crowd hurled rubbish my way, but a few squeezes of my trigger taught them the error of that tactic.

Panting, I wiped blood from my eye. There was a small cut on my forehead, but otherwise I was uninjured.

My gaze swept over the square. It had descended into total chaos, with the barriers knocked prone and both groups swirling about like a horde of angry talusians. The situation had gone from a raucous protest to a full blown riot.

It was possible the arrival of our team might have been the catalyst for the bedlam, but part of me also believed such an outcome was inevitable.

If people want to riot, it doesn't take much to set the spark.

With all of the wild fighting going, on, I could not spot my team.

Only the sound of their weapons discharging gave me an estimate of their location.

But I would have to wade through a sea of hostile humanity in order to reach them.

Skrell.

DOTTIE

After getting such exciting results from the Puppet Master, I'd headed back to Kaster to run the samples through the computers.

And that's where it stopped being exciting.

Things hadn't gone at all the way I wanted them to the night before.

The computers could only handle so much. I'd spent the majority of the day yesterday attempting to develop a new program capable of measuring and quantifying the energy signals from the Puppet Master.

I had a few more ideas to try. I'd definitely have to bribe Kenndrid in engineering.

Again.

Luckily, he had a weak spot the size of Duvest for my double dark chocolate chili brownies.

After I dragged myself home from the lab last night, I baked a fresh batch so I could just warm them up in the oven this morning. Getting them into the basket of my bicycle was a bit of a challenge, since the tin was just a bit too large, and I had to put them in at an angle.

If I was careful, they'd make it to the lab in one piece.

Kenndrid was going to be thrilled. No way he'd refuse my request.

My coworkers always made fun of me for my bike. It wasn't one of the fancy ones most people on this planet had.

It wasn't a hoverbike that ran on solar energy, it was a regular old pedal bike that belonged to my great-great-great grandfather. Maybe there were a few more greats in there, I didn't really know.

It was technically a family heirloom, although I was always replacing parts with new ones, as the ancient ones rusted away.

The bike now looked like a mishmash of aged steel and shiny carbon fiber, and I was fully aware of how ridiculous I looked pedaling through the market district of Kaster.

And I didn't care.

Everyone knew me by the bike. I even had one of those stupid little bells to ring when I passed someone I knew. Which was just about everyone.

When I rode through the market district today, no one waved or smiled as I passed. Instead, everyone was hurriedly packing up their wares and collapsing their stalls.

"What's going on?" I skidded to a stop in front of Hudd's stall. Hudd was an old friend of my family.

"A riot's broken out in the East Quarter."

My stomach sank. The lab was on the other side of the East Quarter.

"I've got to get to the lab," I gasped.

"I wouldn't risk it," Hudd shook his head slowly. "Too much risk of the crazy spilling over."

"I can go the long way around," I insisted. "If nothing else, I have to make sure the lockdown protocols were activated properly. If anything in that lab gets damaged there's no replacing it."

"Be careful."

I nodded to Hudd before pushing off, then turned down one of the back alleys so narrow my handlebars scraped against the wall trying to avoid people.

As I approached the East Quarter, I heard the sounds of the riot. Clashing and shouting. Banging and thumping.

Thankfully, I didn't hear the sounds of blasters.

That was hopeful, right?

I passed a gap in the alleyway leading to the main road. Just as I did, a cluster of fighting humans barreled into me from the side, knocking me off my bike.

In the center of the fight was a red-skinned alien. A Skotan. He threw a punch, knocking out one of the humans attacking him.

This must've been some kind of anti-alien agitators. It made my skin crawl to think anti-alien radicals had made their way into my city.

Aside from my brief conversations with General Rouhr, my contact with the aliens was limited. There were some alien patrols stationed at Kaster but I had no reason to interact with them. My attitude towards the aliens was pretty neutral. I didn't have any alien friends, aside from the Puppet Master.

Though, technically I was the alien in that relationship.

I bore no ill will towards the aliens that now called this planet home.

It was clear to me that they played an integral part in defeating the Xathi, forging an alliance with the Puppet Master, and rebuilding our planet into something better than we humans could've done on our own.

I also knew that many didn't share my mentality. I just thought Kaster was better than that.

I scrambled to my feet after untangling myself from the bike. The Skotan overthrew another one of his attackers but didn't see the man to his back begin to get up.

Not fair!

I dashed forward before I could think twice and kicked the man hard in the jaw.

Instead of a 'thank-you', the Skotan shot me a glare. In the moment of distraction, another man sideswiped me, knocking me to the ground.

The Skotan let out something between a howl and a roar, and I could physically see the rage building up in him.

I only looked away when the man who knocked me to the ground pinned my wrists into the dirt.

"Aren't you a pretty little alien lover," he sneered. Sweat dripped from his hair onto my face. The stench of him made me want to gag.

"Get off me." I wiggled beneath him to no avail.

"Keep doing that," he groaned. "You're getting me excited."

I went still immediately.

From behind the man, the Skotan appeared. His eyes were like fireballs. With one arm, he lifted the man off of me.

With the other, he punched the man in the jaw over and over until blood and teeth splattered on the dust beneath them.

I took the opportunity to scurry away. My ankle

ached, but it wasn't broken. I tried to grab my bike but it'd been damaged when I was sideswiped. The chain was broken. I couldn't use it to get away.

Now what?

More rioters spilled into the narrow alleyway. The Skotan was at a deep disadvantage but he didn't seem to care.

He thrashed about, his blows landing with expert accuracy. He lifted up the rioter that'd pinned me to the ground and threw him into the others. They fell like a house of cards.

I'd never had the opportunity to witness what the aliens could do first hand. I wildly underestimated their physical strength and battle prowess.

I always assumed they were just like humans, only with different skin colors. From afar, that's what they looked like.

That was stupid of me. They weren't just humans in costume.

Now that I had the chance to look at one close up, I noticed the Skotan's arms were covered with sharp armor-like scales. He flexed his muscles and the scales retreated back into his skin.

"Come on," he snarled.

It took me a moment to realize he was addressing me.

Yes, I appreciated that he saved me but he was still trembling with rage. Plus, he was the one the rioters were eager to fight. The last thing I wanted was a target on my back.

"Can you understand me?" He sounded annoyed.

I nodded.

"Then let's go."

"No." My voice wavered as I spoke.

"I wasn't asking," he growled.

He stepped over to me and took me by the arm, his grip firm but not crushing. He tugged my arm, forcing my upper body to come forward. He bent down, put his shoulder to my stomach and lifted me clear off my feet.

Blood rushed to my head as I tipped upside down.

"What the hell are you doing?" I demanded, kicking my legs, despite the pain in one ankle.

My foot made contact with his head. He gripped my foot and firmly pulled it back down into place.

"I'm taking you to safety."

"No place with you is safe!" Great, instead of having a target on my back I was now a target *on his* back.

"Would you rather take your chances on your own?" He demanded. "I could dump you right here and you'd never see me again. I wonder how far you'll get with an injured ankle."

When I didn't say anything, he kept going.

"That male I pulled off of you isn't the only one looking for more than a fight," he warned.

"All right!" I muttered. "Will you at least put me down? I'll come with you."

"Unless you plan on running fast enough to keep up with me, this is the best way to transport you."

"I disagree," I grumbled.

He sped up into a jog. My ribs bumped painfully against the straps of the holsters he wore over his shoulder and my hip bone dug into his shoulder at a bad angle. I sucked in slow breaths. I could put up with this.

It was better than the alternative.

If I twisted my neck to the right, I could see the main road. It was clogged with rioters practically frothing at the mouth.

I wonder what sparked such violence. What was the point of attacking Kaster? All we had was a second-rate lab and an impressive fish market.

Every once in a while, I saw aliens in the crowd. They swung batons and other similar weapons but weren't firing blasters. I assumed that meant they'd been sent to contain the rioters, not to kill them.

In my few brief conversations with General Rouhr, I didn't get the sense that he enjoyed violence. That's probably why the new Nyhiem mayor liked him so much.

However, if all the other aliens had the same mannerisms as the one who now carried me, I could understand some resistance on the part of the humans to making friends.

Riots, however, were not justified. I'd heard on the news about a shooting during the last electoral debate as well as an attack on the building General Rouhr ran his operations from.

Maybe aliens like this Skotan were necessary to bring the violence under control. If Kaster was a target, that meant things were only getting worse.

"Look! He's got a human captive!" One of the rioters on the main road shouted.

"Shit," I swore under my breath.

"Hang on."

"To what?!" I demanded as the Skotan took off in a breakneck sprint. Pain exploded from my hip bone and ribs.

I didn't care. Bruises would heal.

The rioters spilled into the alleyway chasing after us. The Skotan was far too quick. We left them in the dust.

Literally.

He sprinted until we passed two crudely erected barricades. Two aliens held the line with giant blasters. The rioters weren't brave enough to test them.

I looked around even though my view was limited.

The Skotan had brought me to a makeshift base camp.

Well. This was going to be interesting.

JALOK

Behind us, the riot raged on, possibly due to spill our way at any moment.

Ahead, an overturned husk of a land vehicle acted as a bulwark for the rest of Team Three.

Navat spotted my approach and offered a wave. He stood atop the wrecked craft, balancing a belt fed riot control rifle on his hip. I saw Sk'lar barking orders at the rest of the team, shoring up the defenses.

"Jalok." Sk'lar beckoned me over, and I jumped over the makeshift barrier to land in the middle of our hasty defenses. The commander's eyes narrow as he regarded my squealing burden. "Where have you been? And more importantly, what have you done?"

I dropped the woman on the ground, none too

gently as she really pissed me off with all the screaming and squirming.

"Hey." She glared up at me with such indignity that I instantly regretted my decision to drop her.

Not just because I was so taken aback by her fury, but the moment I met her eyes, I could suddenly see the appeal of human mates.

She was worthy of a lusty Skotan song.

A dozen of them.

Her supple body drew my focus my blood began to boil as I took her full beauty in. Hair the color of the afternoon sun cascaded to her shoulders, framing her petite features.

Unfortunately, I didn't have time to apologize to her.

Sk'lar was fuming. "Jalok, I asked you a question."

"Sorry, sir. I was separated from the rest of the team during the riot. Once I was able to get clear of the melee, I spotted this civilian in distress. When I saw the rest of team three gathering, I followed in your wake."

Sk'lar grunted, and squinted at the cut on my forehead.

"You're injured."

"It's nothing. Already coagulated. Besides, none of us have time to fuss over a little blood."

"True enough." Sk'lar looked down at my former passenger. "Are you all right, Ma'am?"

"I'm fine now that this, this *thug* isn't manhandling me."

The little beauty shot me a withering glare.

I tried to pretend that I didn't notice, but her barb stung.

Thug. That's what she thought of me?

"Jalok is a little rough around the edges, but I'm sure he was acting in your best interests. Try to find a safe spot. Things are about to get ugly."

"How you call this a safe spot?" she demanded. "I've been yanked from the street to the middle of a warzone!"

"Do you want to see a real warzone?" I snapped. "Try fighting ten Xathi. Oh right, you saw that when they invaded here, didn't you? And guess who saved you? Us. The same people you're protesting against!"

"I'm not anti-alien!"

"You're not pro-alien either!"

"Can it, you two." Sk'lar came to stand between us. "The enemy is out there, not in here. We need a strategy."

"I'll give you a strategy." I hefted my rifle for emphasis. "Enough latex rounds will take the fight right out of these ignorant hairless apes."

"Hairless apes?" The woman I rescued gaped in indignant disbelief at my words. "More violence isn't the answer we're looking for here."

Navat called from behind me. "Hey, Jalok is an idiot, but I agree that we have to take the offense. We have to act before the riot spreads across the city."

"It might be too late for that." Sk'lar peered out of the dilapidated street we'd claimed as our momentary refuge. The whirlwind of chaos seemed to be getting closer. "Our best bet is to get back to the ship and lift off out of here."

"What? Run away?" I gestured at the riot. "Do you just want to let these animals have the streets?"

"Animals?" Sk'lar glanced at the woman I saved, but I didn't.

"Jalok, can the slurs. Now. We need to get this civilian to safety."

"One human's life versus dozens, maybe hundreds of lives lost during this riot?" I turned to the woman and offered a bow of my head as an apology, since Sk'lar was so sensitive about it. I kept forgetting his girlfriend was a human. "No offense."

"Well, gee, offense has been taken." She gave me a nasty scowl that said bridges had been burnt, collapsed, and sunk into the river.

"Commander."

We all turned in the direction of Navat's bellow. He pointed down the street at a rush of humanity. The anti-alienists had found our refuge.

"At least two dozen adversaries." A projectile

ricocheted off of the vehicle he stood upon. "And some of them have distance weaponry."

"Probably commandeered from civilian security." Sk'lar raised his voice to a shout. "Look alive Team Three. Don't kill unless it's absolutely unavoidable, but hold this position. If we die, she dies."

"Great. More babysitting." Cazak took up a position on the lee side of the wrecked speeder. Tyehn clambered up onto the skeletal remains of a metal staircase. I dragged the woman by the wrist into the burned out interior of the cruiser and crouched behind what used to be a window.

The rest of the team took up cover positions as the anti-alienist's projectiles ricocheted off of our defenses. Sk'lar might be a stick in the mud, but he chose one hell of a defensible position. The rioters had to come to us, with next to no cover available. Unfortunately, there were a lot of them and being overrun was a distinct possibility.

I didn't envy him the command. Far from it. It's hard enough to make split second decisions once the weapons fire is rattling off all around you. It's even harder to take into consideration the whereabouts and wellbeing of an entire strike team. I might gripe about his edicts, but I wasn't going to question him in the heat of battle.

Balancing the end of my rifle across the rusted

window ledge, I took aim at an armed rioter. He had on a similar mask to the grenadiers to protect his identity. My crosshairs fell on his chest, but then I dropped my aim lower, to between his legs. One squeeze of the trigger, and the man doubled over into a mewling heap.

Unfortunately, one of his mates seized up the purloined firearm and started shooting at us anew. The rioters knew we were using non-lethal weaponry, so they charged in fearlessly. But they didn't extend us the same courtesy.

A barrage of projectiles hit Navat's position on top of the wrecked craft. I heard him grunt in pain, then return fire. Half a dozen rioters collapsed on the ground, taken down by his mercy rounds, but I knew he had been hurt.

As if in answer to my thoughts, a hot sticky droplet of blood hit my shoulder. I looked up to see it dripping steadily from a hole in the makeshift roof. I slapped a hand onto my comm unit.

"Sk'lar, Navat's been hit."

A heavy thump from overhead rattled the entire blasted out craft. It seemed the big man went down to one knee.

"I see. Navat, get down from there. Team, give him some cover."

"Oh, I'll give him some cover."

I switched to full automatic and charged out from

under my improvised bunker. Weapons fire ripped through the air all around me, but I stood my ground, splayed my feet and held the rifle at waist height.

The barrel swept across the road, hewing a path through the charging anti-alienists. They fell row by row, not only from my barrage but from the rest of the strike team.

Something streaked past me from behind, and I just caught a glimpse of a gas grenade before it exploded, sending a billowing green cloud over dozens of rioters. The gas was anesthetic designed to render most sapient species unconscious.

For a time, the cloud of gas kept them at bay. Sk'lar called out to the whole team.

"Weapons check."

"I think we're low on ammo all around, Commander." Cazak checked his clip and shook his head. "I've got four rounds left."

"We're out." Navat and Tyehn gestured at their rifles, both flashing the dreaded red rectangle of emptiness.

"I have one more RPG left, and a few shots in my sidearm." Sk'lar peered out over the mist. "Heads up, they're coming in again. All right. So it's going to be melee combat."

Sk'lar looked at Navat, who had sprayed medi-gel to heal his wounds temporarily. "Are you well, Navat?"

"Fit to fight, Commander." Navat gave a thumbs up,

but the edge of pain in his voice was impossible to ignore.

Cazak picked up a street sign knocked asunder by passing rioters. He turned it around so the chunk of concrete clinging to the base acts as the head of a club. I winced, because I knew that improvised cudgel was going to be lethal in application.

Sk'lar wasn't exactly pushing us to use non-lethal force any longer, however. We all knew that the time for that was past. We'd been exercising restraint, only using the bare minimum of force to protect ourselves.

That was about to change. In my heart, I felt a swell of pity for those anti-alienists. They'd hurt one of our own, two of our own if I counted the gash on my forehead. My scales popped out to the surface, and a guttural growl began low in my throat.

Come forward, you bigoted men of Ankou I thought. *Come forward, and face Strike Team Three when we're no longer trying to play nice. We are killers of Xathi. See what we make of your soft skins. Come forward, and let us send you to whatever afterlife awaits your kind.*

Come.

DOTTIE

I think I'd gone into some kind of shock. Weird.

I'd never gone into shock in my life. I'd never felt what I was now feeling before in my life either.

I'd hypothesize that shock and whatever I was feeling now were one and the same.

That made sense, right?

One moment, I'd been unceremoniously dumped on the ground by Jalok the dickhead- I mean, Skotan.

The next, they were all rushing off toward something likely dangerous. I had no desire to be a part of that.

"Get in there!" Jalok didn't so much as order me as he did shoved me underneath an overturned transport.

I put my weight on the upside down seat, hoping to steady myself but it nearly collapsed under my weight.

I refused to believe that Jalok or any member of his team sat on these. If it couldn't bear my weight, no way in hell could it support one of the aliens. Even the smallest of them was basically a titan.

I wish I knew what was going on at the lab. The riot seemed to be moving in the opposite direction but when has a riot ever been predictable?

The heat was oppressive. If anything, it was only making me feel worse. From what Jalok said, the rioters were moving closer to the makeshift camp.

If I was careful, I could sneak away which would put me closer to the lab. I'd be out of Jalok's hair and better able to protect my work.

I stumbled back out from under the transport and sucked in the fresh air.

Then immediately choked on the dust stirred up by the aliens and rioters. A rioter collapsed at my feet. His hand was broken and bleeding. I stumbled around him.

My brain wasn't working as fast as it normally did.

I was out of my element here. Way out of my element. If I was going to get out of this unscathed, I needed to let go of my fear and rely on logic.

I was good with logic. One step at a time, right?

I looked around the camp. Many of the aliens were fighting rioters' hand to hand. Some of them had batons. The one thing I didn't hear was gunfire or blasters discharging. I wasn't likely to be hit by a stray bullet.

Now, I just had to figure out which direction the lab was in from where I was now.

As it turns out, an active battlefield isn't the best place to come up with a detailed escape plan.

Another rioter saw me and charged at me with a thick, rusty knife at the ready.

No time for logic now.

I had to run.

I ran blindly through the fighting, knocking into any rioter I could. I liked to think I was helping but that probably wasn't true.

At some point, the rioter chasing me was taken out by an alien. I didn't look back to see who it was. I had to find a place to hide and wait this out.

All I wanted was to get to my lab. Was that so much to ask?

I spied an industrial dumpster that had been pulled over to construct part of a barricade between the base camp and the city streets.

It was too tall for me to jump into but there was a large gap between the bottom of the dumpster and the ground. With no better options in sight, I dropped onto my belly and rolled under.

It took some wiggling, but I got myself into a position where I could watch the fight unfold.

The only advantage the riots had were their numbers but that didn't appear to be doing them any favors. The aliens outmatched them in size, strength, stamina, combat techniques and tons of other attributes I didn't know enough about to comment on like the club-thingy one of the Skotan's wielded.

It wasn't Jalok. He didn't have a club like that.

I would've noticed that when I was thrown over his shoulder.

This Skotan had electric currents running through the wooden club. I wondered how he did that without completely frying the wood. The effects were devastating. When the club made contact with the jaw of a rioter, it left deep purple scars that looked like lightning bolts on his skin.

The other nearby rioters took note of their comrade's damaged face and took decisive steps away from the Skotan with the club. Wise choice. At least the rioters weren't completely stupid. Just mostly stupid.

The Valorni, green aliens with purple stripes down their arms, didn't seem to carry much in the way of weapons.

Instead they used brute force to subdue the rioters that challenged them. I watched in awe as a single Valorni lifted three rioters off their feet with one arm and launched them into a tent structure.

A K'ver came into view. Like the Valorni, he didn't

carry any weapons that I could see. However, instead of launching anyone who came his way across the camp, he engaged in complicated hand-to-hand moves that left me, as well as anyone he was fighting, dizzy.

The K'ver moved so quickly his opponent couldn't keep up with him. I felt the urge to laugh as the rioter swung blindly at the K'ver. When the K'ver was done disorienting his opponent, he knocked him out with a swift punch.

As I watched the aliens fight, the anxiety knotted in my stomach started to ease. What I still couldn't figure out was why Kaster? The only reason that made sense to me was that the anti-alien radicals were trying to make some kind of statement.

Maybe they wanted Nyhiem to see how wide-spread they were or how powerful they were. Anyone could've told them that was a losing battle.

A rioter landed limp in the dust a few yards from my dumpster-slash-shelter as if to further punctuate my point.

I doubt the anti-alien radicals ever intended for it to go this far. Things likely snowballed out of control into this clusterfuck.

Five rioters caught my attention. They looked like they were running away from something rather than into battle. They kept looking over their shoulders, their faces pale and covered in dust and blood.

Jalok appeared in a cloud of dust hot on their tails. I saw the rage burning in his eyes even from my position under the dumpster.

Even though his anger wasn't turned on me, a cold sheet of fear settled over my body. Just seeing him like that made me want to shrink into a tiny ball and hide, yet I couldn't look away.

He caught up to the slowest rioter of the group. Judging by the rioter's uneven walk, Jalok had already done some damage to his kneecap.

Jalok punched the rioter square in the spine. I heard a sickening crunch. The rioter fell to the ground. He wasn't dead but it didn't look like he could move.

I thought I'd seen Jalok fight when we collided in the alleyway.

I was wrong. He was just warming up then. He caught up to the next rioter and yanked him back by his hair.

Jalok placed his other hand around the rioter's throat until he went limp. At first, I thought he was dead but after he hit the ground, I saw the slow rise and fall of his chest.

It was strange how Jalok could be an unstoppable fighting machine but also be careful enough not to kill if he didn't have to.

Incapacitation seemed to be his goal. The only rioter he'd killed that I knew of was the one that pinned me down in the alleyway. I couldn't say I felt bad for the guy.

Two of the rioters managed to get out of Jalok's warpath by splitting up and running in other directions. Unfortunately, the remaining rioter was stupidly brave. He turned and faced Jalok with only a metal pole to defend himself.

Jalok disarmed him in seconds.

It was almost comical.

"And you wonder why we want you all dead," the rioter sneered.

Jalok closed the distance between them and picked the rioter up by the collar with two hands.

"You attack a town unprovoked and wonder why I showed up?" He snarled.

"We weren't unprovoked. We wanted the aliens stationed here gone. We won't be silenced."

"You will be silenced if your plan is to keep harming innocent people just trying to make a living," Jalok snarled "All you're doing is making things harder for your own species, a species I've sworn to protect. I will do whatever I have to in order to keep that promise."

Despite the unsavory context, Jalok's words struck me as honorable.

"Go ahead and kill me then. Isn't that what you aliens are at heart? Killers." The rioter spat on Jalok's face.

"I'm not going to kill you," Jalok replied with a calmness that was somehow more terrifying than anger. "But I am going to break every bone in your body."

I looked away for this part.

But with each scream of the rioter, I knew Jalok was keeping his word.

JALOK

A squirming mass of limbs rained ineffectual blows down upon my scaled hide as I lifted the two rioters into the air.

Amidst the carnage of the battlefield, looking for the perfect place to deposit my burden, I felt alive.

This was what I was made for.

The angry shouts of Tyehn drew my attention. He was fending off a half dozen rioters armed with makeshift weapons.

Under normal circumstances, the big Valorni would have finished them off with ease. Injured as he was, however, the numbers game overwhelmed him.

With a shout, I sent the struggling men in my arms sailing through the air. My meat missiles crashed into the throng and sent rioters sprawling. Tyehn used the distraction to smash two rioter's skulls together with a sound akin to a hard shelled fruit split open.

Shrieking sirens heralded the arrival of reinforcements to our location.

Finally. After things were pretty much over. The men who rushed our position now lay in various miserable heaps about the street.

Most of them weren't even conscious, and those that were probably wish that they were not, like the fellow with his knee bent the wrong way courtesy of a blow from Cousin Cazak's makeshift club.

I'd done just as much mayhem with my bare hands, though, if not more.

As security filled the street and took in the brutality of Team Three's prowess, they quickly called for emergency medical technicians—but not for us.

For our victims.

Cazak staggered over to me, blood covering him but most of it not his own. He slammed the crimson spattered concrete cudgel head first to the ground, crossed his arms, and grinned.

"Twelve being stretchered out." He jerked his head toward a human groaning on a gurney.

"I can't feel my legs—I can't feel my legs."

"Huh." I shrugged casually. "I lost count at fourteen, but it's not like it's a competition, right cousin?"

"Fourteen? Ludicrous. You just picked a number higher than mine."

"Really" I jabbed my thumb at the stack of unconscious rioters near where Tyehn stood. "There's three right there. Then there's the guy with his jaw dislocated over there, and that human with the large belly draped over the sewage vent, and--"

"All right, I get the point. Well fought, Jalok."

"Well fought, Cazak."

We bumped fists, and then I noticed a sharp pain in my back. Turning my head, I could just make out a shard of metal stuck between two scales on my shoulder blade.

"Damn it." I turned around and present my back to Cazak. "Yank this out, will you?"

"Sure thing." He took hold of the shard, and I clamped down on a scream as he gave it a hard yank.

Cazak staggered back, and I straightened up, back in flaming agony.

"Did you get it?"

"Not all of it." He showed me the bloody piece of shrapnel. "Part of it is stuck up under the bone. You're going to need someone to cut it out, cousin."

"Great." I moved my arm about carefully to test his hypothesis, and was rewarded by an intense pain. "Damn. Just don't tell Sk'lar or he'll send me off to the quacks before I get a chance to bust more heads."

"Don't tell me what?"

Gritting my teeth, I turned around to stare into the jet black features of the leader of Team Three.

"Jalok's been injured, sir,"

"Thanks, Cazak."

"Hmm." Sk'lar assessed the wound on my back. "That's pretty deep. Report to the medical center, soldier."

"But Sk'lar--"

"That's an order. I'll expect clearance from a medical professional before you can return to duty."

"Yes, sir." Shooting Cazak a withering glare, I stalked off toward the medical transport hovercraft.

The technicians slapped a bandage on to stop the constant seep of blood and directed me to climb into the back. I just happened to wind up sitting next to one of the men I'd injured during the riot.

"Oh no, not him. Get him away from me, get him away--"

"Boo."

The man wet himself, which, while quite funny in the moment, made the ride to the medical center rather unpleasant.

Even the EMTs, used to various gushing bodily fluids, were bitching about the smell.

It was still funny.

Because my condition wasn't life threatening, I got

sent to what amounted to the rear of the line. Once the triage nurse assessed me, she decided with her vast medical knowledge of my species that the shrapnel sat dangerously close to an artery.

Thus, I ended up being ordered to sit in a bed holding a bandage in place with one hand while I awaited a surgeon.

"That looks painful."

Turning to my left, I found that my day had gotten even worse.

Or better.

The rush of emotions was confusing, uneasy.

Sitting in the bed next to mine, her leg bandaged heavily, was the strawberry blonde human woman who nearly got me killed with her screaming and squirming.

Maybe she'd let me take her out later. There was something compelling about her, despite how she argued with everything I said.

"It's nothing for a Skotan warrior." I attempted to shrug, but that drove the shrapnel in deeper and I couldn't hold in a wince.

"Well, 'nothing' looks pretty painful. Don't worry, those painkillers they're feeding into your arm should kick in soon. Myself, I'm experiencing the most amazing display of vibrating blue abstract shapes in my peripheral vision."

"Sounds like a personal problem," I tried to joke. I wasn't good at this. Whatever this was.

I turned my head away and tried to talk to the attending physicians so I wouldn't have to speak to her. However, they were called away on an emergency and left me alone with the woman and these uncertain...feelings.

"I got hurt too. That riot was just insane. One second, it's loud but contained, and the next boom. People running and fighting everywhere."

"Bah. It's nothing compared to the chaos of a battlefield against real soldiers. That untrained mob went down without much of a fight."

"Managed to get you pretty good, though."

My scales popped out and I gave her a good, low growl.

Then she laughed. She actually laughed. Even Cazak shuts his mouth when I do a full on intimidation display.

"That's a cute trick." Cute? "Hey, don't feel bad. I saw you fighting in that alley. You were amazing, like doing red raptor spinning ju jitsu. It was incredible."

She was baffling...but she wasn't wrong. I really did crack some heads during that brawl.

"All Skotan must learn the arts of unarmed combat. I was the champion of my age group seven times."

"That's cool. I'm not much for fighting. I'm a scientist."

"Really?" I asked, grateful for a small lead in the conversation. "I don't suppose you study weaponry or munitions?"

"No, my specialty is environmental sciences."

Oh. Nothing I knew anything about, then.

She continued. "But lately, I've been working with the Puppet Master. Did you know he's as old as the planet? A minute to him is probably a thousand years to us."

Now she did have my attention.

Like just about everyone dwelling on this planet, I had a lot of curiosity about the Puppet Master. The idea of a hyper intelligent, gigantic plant being the literal core of the planet was very relevant information to anyone who lives here.

"Does it—does it speak to you? In words?"

"Well, yes. I suppose it does, in a way."

"It speaks your human tongue?"

"It speaks telepathically, so I think I hear it in my own tongue because that's how my mind interprets it. If he spoke to you, you might hear it in Skotan."

"Hmm." That was interesting.

Skrell. She was interesting.

"I'm Dottie, by the way. Well, Doctor Dorothy Bellin

but *don't* call me Dorothy. Only my Mom gets away with that sin, and only because I can't seem to stop her."

She thrust out her hand for the human ritual of shaking, but I grimaced and held my shoulder.

"I have this—that is, this thing is--"

"Oh, right, sorry." She winced in sympathy and retracted her hand. "What's your name?"

"Jalok, son of Kronuz."

"Well, it's nice to meet you, Jalok. I guess."

I ignored her odd expression as footsteps approached in the hall.

"Oh thank goodness."

A pair of medics entered the room, bearing a rolling cart with them. The cart contained a magnetic resonance device which pinpointed the shrapnel in my shoulder. Then it used a magnet to precisely withdraw it.

I gasped when it ripped out my back. The doctors quickly applied a spray of cellular regenerative paste.

"There you go, big guy." The doctor patted me on my good shoulder. "With your metabolism, you'll be mostly healed by the time you check out at the front desk."

"My thanks." I stood up and smiled, genuinely in a good mood after talking with this beautiful creature. "Dottie was it? It was nice to meet you."

"Nice to meet you--" the doors swung shut behind

me as the physicians attended to her leg. They had taken over and whatever my brain was doing when I was around her wasn't my problem anymore.

I couldn't repress the little jaunty strut in my stride as I headed for the front desk to get my medical clearance.

I had helped quell a riot, personally sent over a dozen miscreants to the hospital, and rescued a beautiful and probably at least somewhat useful science type person.

All in all, a good day's work.

Once I signed out at the front desk, I headed for the exit. Of all the people I didn't expect to see, my cousin Cazak was standing in the lobby, leaning against the wall and looking bored. He perked up at my approach.

"Cousin, it's so kind of you to check on my wellbeing, but I'm fine."

"Oh, that's right, you got a little scratch back there. Well, I didn't come to check on you. This was where central command told me to find you."

"Why you? Didn't they think I suffered enough from the injury?"

"Nope." He slapped a datapad against my chest. "I'm here to deliver your new temporary orders, and was told to do so immediately."

"Great, as long as it gets me away from that little human woman." I pulled up the info on the datapad while Cazak gave me a big shit eating grin. "Protect the scientist in charge of attending to the Puppet Master until a permanent bodyguard is assigned...no, it couldn't be."

Then I noticed the name of my charge, the person I was supposed to escort back to her lab.

Dr. Dorothy Bellin.

Dottie.

DOTTIE

"I wish you'd stop grumbling," I called over my shoulder as Jalok and I left the compound.

He had done everything but sitting on the ground and refusing to move.

How could he be seven feet tall and as big as a tree, and act like a toddler?

"I haven't said anything."

"I can feel your displeasure radiating from you," I shot back.

I wasn't happy about this arrangement either. I was glad to have a bodyguard for the moment.

I didn't think of it during the riot, but it would've been terrible if I'd fallen into the hands of the rioters for more than one reason.

Obviously, the man who pinned me made it clear

what he wanted but it was the knowledge I possessed that was far too valuable to put at risk.

I should've been assigned a bodyguard the moment I got the job working with the Puppet Master. The anti-alien radicals had already attacked him more than once.

That didn't mean I wanted Jalok following me everywhere.

I'd admit that there was a moment when the rioters were in the camp that I thought Jalok honorable in his dedication to protecting innocents.

However, that single moment didn't cancel out his overall jerk-ness or the fact that he could kill a grown man with a flick of his wrist.

As one of the aforementioned innocents, I knew I was safe from Jalok's wrath. But what if he mistook one of the Puppet Master's vines as a threat and sheared it off? What if the Puppet Master didn't want to talk to me when Jalok was around?

"Are you an empath?"

"Beg pardon?" I cast a confused look over my shoulder.

"A human with the ability to sense the feelings of others."

"I don't think that's a thing."

"It is, indeed," he insisted. "I've met an empath. Her name is Jeneva. She is now under the employment of General Rouhr."

"How lovely." I faced forward once more.

"I only ask because being an empath is useful. I've yet to see how you're useful to General Rouhr all the way out here."

I bit the inside of my cheek in an attempt to keep my temper from flaring. This bodyguard arrangement was only going to be tolerable if we weren't at each other's throats the whole time. Clearly, it was up to me to prevent that from happening.

"Good thing it's not your job to determine my usefulness."

"Lucky for you as well."

"What is your problem?" I groaned through clenched teeth. So much for keeping the peace.

"I don't want to be here."

Well, at least he was honest.

"I don't want you here either. You're going to disrupt my work which General Rouhr, your boss, thinks is vital. Why don't you crawl on back to camp?"

"And shirk my duties? I'd rather bathe in icthiannous goo."

"I don't even want to know what that is."

"It's the viscous secretions from a creature on my home planet."

"I said I didn't want to know."

"You said you're a scientist. I assumed that meant

you want to know everything." He was taunting me, trying to push my buttons.

"I'm working on trying to understand my own planet at the moment. We're occupied by a giant plant that's actually a sentient being, and apparently even he has a further mystery known as the 'Ancient Enemies.' Once I get all of that squared away you can tell me all about the gooey creature that lives on yours."

"It isn't gooey. It secretes goo. Big difference."

At long last, I reached the lab. I swiped my ID card at the entrance, contemplating letting the door close before Jalok could follow me inside.

The security light flashed red in response to my ID. I frowned and tried again only to be rejected once more.

"Clearly you're a very important person," Jalok chuckled.

"Are all Skotan this coarse and rude or did I just get lucky?" I snapped.

After the third swipe, an alarm went off. One of my associates, Eluna, came rushing to shut the alarm off and open the door for me.

"Sorry about that, Dottie. The scanner took some damage earlier today. It didn't let me in either," she explained in a rush. Her gaze shifted from me to Jalok. Her expression changed from one of concern to one of interest.

"And who's this?" She asked. "Does he have clearance?"

"No, but he's been assigned to guard me for today."

"On that secret, special mission for the General?" Her voice dropped to a whisper that wasn't as quiet as she believed it was.

"Yes," I chuckled. "Having him here is going to be a real treat."

"Allow me to introduce myself." Jalok stepped around me to offer his hand to Eluna. When she shook it, he lowered his head to kiss the top of her hand.

"Oh my!" Eluna blushed deep crimson. "It's an honor to have you with us."

"It's an honor to be here. Everyone here is so valuable to General Rouhr and our mission. I'm excited to learn something new."

Eluna, still holding Jalok's hand, turned back to me.

"Are all the aliens this nice?" She gushed.

"Not that I know of." My cheeks ached from forcing a smile. "Sorry, Eluna but I have to check my data. That means the big red guy has to come with me."

"Shame." Her eyes roved over his body. I could tell Jalok enjoyed the attention. "Hope to see you around."

"You will."

Once we were safely in my office with the door locked, I whirled on him.

"Would you mind telling me what the hell that was?"

"I can't be polite to a new person?"

"You only did that to look like an angel when I go around telling everyone how insufferable you are."

"If you weren't correct, I'd tell you that you sound paranoid." Jalok leaned back on my desk and folded his arms across his chest.

"Stop smirking like that."

"Make me."

Tension hung in the air between us as I tried, and failed, to come up with a witty comeback. Scowling, I pushed past Jalok to get to my personal console. From there, I was able to determine if any of the lab's equipment was damaged from the riots. Luckily, everything had been spared.

For the first time since I went down that stupid alleyway, I allowed myself to take a deep breath.

"Good sigh or bad sigh?" Jalok asked.

"It's a none of your business sigh." What I wouldn't give for a moment alone simply to process everything that I'd been through this morning. I wanted to talk to the Puppet Master for the rest of the day but that wasn't on the agenda.

"If you're planning on blankly staring at your console all day, can I at least have a chair?"

I jerked my chin toward the spare chair near the door.

"I'd ask you if all humans are as coarse and as rude

as you are but I already know the answer to that." Jalok settled himself into the chair. It was too small for him. He struggled to find a comfortable way to sit.

"I'm done talking to you for the next six hours," I announced.

"Why? All out of comebacks?"

"No, I have to do work for your boss." That appeared to shut him up. I relished the silence. Since I stepped out of my apartment that morning, I haven't had a moment of silence. Even with Jalok in the room, it was easy for me to sink into my work.

Hours passed in the blink of an eye. I'd actually gotten somewhere with analyzing the data from the Puppet Master, which was an unexpected surprise.

I still had to send some to the lab in Nyhiem for further analysis, though. Getting those results back was something to look forward to.

With all of this bodyguard talk, I wasn't sure when I'd be allowed to go visit the Puppet Master.

"I've finished my work," I announced to Jalok, who'd dozed off in the chair. He woke with a start and reached for the weapon at his side before realizing that there was no danger. He cleared his throat and got to his feet.

"I am to escort you home when you're ready."

"Give me five minutes to tidy up," I nodded.

"But," he looked around my office, "everything's already spotless."

"You and I have a different definition of spotless."

Jalok made various impatient and annoyed grunts and groans while I tidied up and made sure everything was in its proper place for tomorrow. He was raring to go when I finished.

"What's got you in such a hurry?" I asked as we waited for the lift.

"Once you're home the night guard takes over," he explained. "I get to go do whatever I want."

"And what do you want?" I asked.

"I don't know. This town doesn't have much by way of entertainment."

"I have to agree with you on that," I laughed.

"I might die of shock."

"Don't make promises you can't keep."

Jalok let out a barking laugh.

"Not bad."

"Which way to the alley you found me in?" I asked once we were a block away from the lab.

"That's not the fastest way to get you home." Jalok lifted a brow.

"I know but I left my bike in the alley and I want to take it home. I can probably fix it," I explained.

"There could be rioters lingering in the dark alleys. They probably dragged your bike off for parts, anyway."

"Can we please go check? It's been in the family for ages. It's from Earth."

"Are you going to keep bringing it up if we don't?"

"Yes. I'll be incredibly annoying and never let you forget it. Besides, I have some brownies in there you might like."

"Fine." Jalok groaned and altered our course.

My bike was still in the alley though it was in desperate need of care. I wouldn't be riding it any time soon.

And those brownies were long gone.

At least I made my great-great-great grandad proud by coming back for it. I reached to pick it up but Jalok swung it over his shoulder with surprising gentleness.

"We'll move quicker if I carry it," he grunted.

I didn't argue.

There was a Valorni stationed outside of my apartment complex when we arrived. He and Jalok exchanged a few words.

"Have a good night." Jalok tipped his head to be before sauntering off, leaving me to carry my bike up three flights of stairs.

Jerk.

JALOK

I hesitated in front of Sk'lar's office door, my hand inches away from the chime as the morning sun splashed warmth across my back. The rumors I'd heard from my teammates said that my actions during the riot had come under scrutiny.

It seems that not all of the rioters I put down had recovered, and some never would.

Inside, I knew that I was just acting in self-defense, and defense of my team. But that kind of attitude never goes over well with the brass. So I had to gather up all of my mental faculties and prepare for an intense grilling without taking it personally.

Still, I stood in the hallway like a fool. Several attaches passed me by, giving me puzzled looks. At that point, I'd have rather stepped in front of a charging

Xathi than walk into that ready room to face the music, to use a human term.

At last, I shoved my finger onto the chime and waited. The door slid aside, and Sk'lar glanced up from the datapad in his hand.

The ebon skinned commander sat behind a glossy desk he rarely had time to use. His face was inscrutable, so I had no clues about what was in store for me.

"Jalok." He gestured to the seat across from him. "Please sit down."

I arched an eyebrow at his unexpected manners. Sk'lar wasn't known for being articulate or gentlemanly.

My bulk settled into the chair, which elicited creaking protests. Once I was ready, Sk'lar punched buttons on his console.

"You and I are going to have a conference call with the General, Vrehx and Karzin."

"I see, sir."

Sk'lar glanced sharply at me, then completed the call.

"Try to accept your recriminations with some dignity. Your behavior reflects on all of Team Three."

"Understood, sir."

He caught the sharp edge to my tone, and fixed me with a worried frown until we heard the general's gruff tone over the comms.

"General Rouhr here."

"General, it's Sk'lar."

"Ah, good. Vrehx and Karzin are in attendance. Is Jalok there yet?"

"Present and accounted for, sir."

"Hmph." I could hear the disdain heavy in the general's voice. "Jalok, I certainly hope you have an explanation for your overzealous application of force during the unpleasantness in Kaster."

I leaned back in my chair and crossed my arms over my chest defiantly.

"You mean the riot? Riots are unpleasant, but I wouldn't refer to them as unpleasantness. I'd refer to them as damn near a battle field."

"Your tone is inappropriate, Jalok." Sk'lar's reprimand hung in the air until I heard Vrehx laugh.

"Let him speak in his own words, Commander Sk'lar. Allow Jalok enough rope to hang himself with."

"A curious metaphor, sir, given that Skotan neck muscles are too thick and powerful for such an execution method to be effective. Sir."

Sk'lar's eyes widened, and an incredulous expression stretched his ebon features. There's silence on the other end, and then General Rouhr let out a great guffaw.

"Oh, I like this one. He has spunk."

"General, please, this is meant to be an inquiry, not an endorsement of his character."

"You are correct, Karzin. My apologies."

"Jalok, you are here today because we have found your actions to be unbecoming of a strike team soldier." Sk'lar really hammed it up for the General. "The force you used was inappropriate for the situation."

"Inappropriate?" I scoffed. "I was out of ammunition, and had no melee weaponry. Hand to hand was my only choice."

"We were being rushed by a group of armed rioters, and Navat had been shot." Sk'lar was putting on a show for the brass, but he was also trying to mitigate how much trouble I would get in. "Team Three was forced to use whatever methods happened to be available."

"Whatever methods available?" Vrehx's voice was ripe with derision. "Would that include smashing a man's skull into the pavement?"

I shrugged.

"He was trying to kill me."

"What about the poor fellow whose back has been broken, and will need months of rehab to walk again?"

"I didn't know that humans bent backward that easily. My mistake."

Sk'lar seemed ready to explode. Maybe that wasn't the right answer.

Karzin interjected. "I'm more concerned about his unscheduled dentistry."

I cocked my head to the side, because I wasn't sure what the leader of Strike Team Two was referring to. "Sir?"

Sk'lar cleared his throat. When he spoke, his tone dripped with anger. "I believe they are referring to the man whose bottom row of teeth you broke off at the gumline."

"He tried to bite me. Stupid move for a species without carnivorous jaws."

"Enough." General Rouhr's snarl cut off all debate. "We are not here to argue with you, Jalok. Obviously you believe your actions were not grounds for discipline—"

"It was self-defense."

"—but it is not your opinion that matters here. We believe you have acted with unnecessary violence toward the civilian populace."

"The same populace that was protesting my right to exist? That civilian—"

"Shut. Up." Sk'lar clamped his hand down on my forearm with a vice like grip. "Please continue, General. There will be no further interruptions."

Sk'lar glared at me for emphasis, and released my arm.

"Thank you, Commander. Jalok, you are a skilled

and powerful warrior. We value your contributions highly, but you must learn to exercise restraint. The humans, even the ones who are uncomfortable with our presence, are not our enemies."

The general's words hung in the air, and sparked a memory.

"Ah, General, I need a moment of your time."

"This hearing is not over yet, soldier."

"I know, but this is important. I'm not trying to distract you from the matter at hand, I promise."

General Rouhr leaned back in his seat, sighed and steepled his hands before his breast. "What's on your mind, Jalok?"

"You remember that hysterical human I had to escort back to her lab?"

"Dr. Dottie Bellin is her name, not Hysterical Human."

"Sorry, Vrehx. Dr. Bellin, as you may know, has been communicating with the Puppet Master. Apparently, they're really friendly. He told her about something he called 'ancient enemies.'"

"Ancient enemies?" Sk'lar frowned, and shook his bald head. "That doesn't sound appealing in the least."

"Who in the world would want a gigantic hyper intelligent plant as an enemy?"

"I'm not certain, Karzin.," the general said slowly.

"But I know someone who might provide us with a clue. Wait a moment while I contact Fen."

As the leader of the Urai and controller of the rift technology, Fen was brought in whenever issues arose that required a deep knowledge of the cosmos.

But once Fen was patched into our conference call, she doesn't provide much help.

"I have heard legends about an ancient, predatory race," she answered, after I relayed the brief words Dottie had said, beginning to think I shouldn't have brought it up. "They were already infamous before the most ambitious of our species had yet discovered interstellar travel."

"Do you have any idea of what they are, Fen? Or what possible threat they might pose to the Puppet Master?" General Rouhr's tone was worried, but not terribly so.

"Not to mention us, General."

"I'm afraid not. The legends are just that—vague on details but full of grisly mentions of doom and despair. I'll keep working on it."

She disappeared from the call.

"So glad we called in the expert," I muttered under my breath.

"What was that, soldier?"

I smiled at Sk'lar and gave him a salute. "Nothing, sir. Am I dismissed?"

"Not so fast." I could hear the disapproval in Vrehx's tone. "There is still the little matter the consequences of your inexcusable violence during the riot."

"Oh, so now you're calling it a riot..." Sk'lar shook his head, eyes narrowed to slits, and I cut myself off.

"Not to mention your inhospitable treatment of Dr. Bellin."

"But I saved her life!"

"And created a terrible impression upon her of both the military and the Skotan species as a whole. Your tone indicates you have learned nothing today. I am afraid you might not be fit for duty, Jalok."

That statement sent a stab of panic through me.

Not fit for duty? What was I supposed to do? Get a job as a farmer?

"Sir, let's not be too hasty." Sk'lar glanced over at me, and though there was derision in his gaze a slight smile played at his lips. "Jalok needs to learn self-discipline, but there's no other soldier I'd rather have guarding my flank than him."

I did a double take. Sk'lar was not often a font of flowing praise.

"General Rouhr." I did not like the crafty tone in Sk'lar's voice. "I think there may be a way to provide an object lesson to Jalok, and give him an opportunity to learn self-control."

"Go on."

I tried to ignore the sinking feeling in my chest.

"Dr. Bellin is still in need of a full time bodyguard, is she not?"

"What?" I stood up and stared down at him with disbelief. "No."

"Yes." Sk'lar glared up at me firmly, but then a satisfied grin spread over his features. "I would like to recommend that Jalok be assigned to said duty. It would be a great opportunity for him."

"I concur." General Rouhr sounded as if he were enjoying my misery just a little too much. "This is an excellent solution for both problems."

Fuming, I glanced from the console to my commanding officer, but found no respite in either the cold metal or his colder demeanor.

"Don't I get a say in this?"

"No. You are dismissed, Jalok. Report to Dr. Bellin immediately for duty first thing in the morning. Stay with her. That is all."

I managed to get all the way down the hall from his office before I started cursing.

But I headed for Bellin's lab anyway.

Bodyguard duty was not what a soldier wanted to do.

But being around a beautiful human woman?

I could get used to that easily.

DOTTIE

I was woken up by a sharp knock at my door.

I knew without opening my eyes that it was Jalok.

"You're running late!" He shouted through the door.

Who even let him up to my floor? He was going to wake up my neighbors.

I laid still and silent in my bed. Perhaps if I didn't answer, he'd think I already went to the lab and leave me alone. Of course, I had no such luck. He just kept on banging away like he was getting paid per knock.

I put my pillow over my face and let out a frustrated scream.

Since the riot broke out, General Rouhr and the associates that oversaw the running of my lab agreed that I was not to venture into an area that couldn't be secured.

That included the crater at the old *Vengeance* crash site I'd been working out of for the last week.

I'd analyzed the last of my data yesterday, aside from what I sent over to the Nyhiem lab to be elaborated on.

Today, I had nothing to do but twiddle my thumbs and wait around.

I hated waiting on someone else so I could continue my work.

It made no sense to keep me from returning to the Puppet Master. If anything, the Puppet Master should be my bodyguard.

Not Jalok the Skotan with a hot temper and no manners.

Even if he did make something, deep in my belly, flutter.

Just a bit.

I could ignore it.

"Dottie, I swear on my life I will break this door down!" Jalok hollered.

Probably.

"I swear on my life that I'll break your neck if you don't knock that off right now, young man!" The crackly old voice of Mrs. Robin made me chuckle.

She had to be over one hundred by now and I fully believed her when she said she'd break Jalok's neck. She might only be five feet tall but she could aim that cane of hers with deadly accuracy.

I climbed out of bed to knock on the wall I shared with her apartment.

"No need, Mrs. Robin. He's government property. I wouldn't want you getting in trouble."

"If you say so, dearie. Let me know if you change your mind! That riot sure did put a fire in my belly!"

I laughed into the palm of my hand and went to the front door. I opened it to find a very impatient Jalok taking up my entire doorway.

"You're running late," he growled.

"No, I'm not. I'm going at the pace I want to go. And what are you doing here anyway?"

"I'm your bodyguard," he snapped. "Again."

"What? Why?"

Jalok opened his mouth to say something but quickly closed it.

"What?"

"Are you planning to get dressed this morning?"

I looked down in horror to see that I was still wearing the tank top and panties I'd worn to bed.

"Excuse me." I walked back to my bedroom with as much dignity as I could measure. I was dressed and back in the main room in less than a minute.

"You're still blushing," Jalok teased.

"Is there any way I could convince you not to accompany me to work?"

"Is it because I saw you in your undergarments?" Jalok gave me a knowing look.

"No. What are we? Twelve?" I rolled my eyes and scoffed. "It's because your presence is detrimental to my work."

"Look, I'm not happy about this arrangement either. I have more important things to do than babysit someone who doesn't want my help."

"So, why don't we make a case to General Rouhr or my bosses?" I suggested.

"If you want to give that a go, by all means." Jalok lifted his hands up and stepped out of my doorframe.

"Have you already asked?" I stepped by him into the narrow hallway.

"A soldier doesn't simply ask his General to be reassigned if he doesn't like the job," Jalok replied.

"What's all the noise at this ungodly hour?" Mr. Falcone, the neighbor across from me, threw his door open. Wearing nothing but a white undershirt, blue boxers, and thick white tube socks, he fixed Jalok with a glare.

"Is this gentleman bothering you, little lady?" Mr. Falcone snarled.

"On the contrary, I've been assigned to protect her," Jalok replied.

Oh god. Could this get any worse?

"Everything's fine, Mr. Falcone. Go back to your morning shows," I urged my neighbor. Mr. Falcone closed his door with a grunt.

"You live in a very active building," Jalok muttered.

"We're kind of like a family. A mismatched, dysfunctional one but a family nonetheless."

Jalok caught the attention of three other neighbors on our way down. He dismissed the night guard at the front of my apartment complex before we set on our way to the lab.

When we reached the lab, Eluna was waiting in the entry room. She tried to hide it, but her whole face lit up when she saw me and Jalok approach.

"If you talk to her, please don't lead her on," I warned Jalok. "If she develops feelings for you, it's going to suck for her when you get reassigned."

"I'll try not to be irresistible and charming."

Jerk.

"You're already doing a sensational job. I'm going to talk to the bosses."

"Good luck."

Since my immediate superior was lost to us during the Xathi invasion, the three partners who owned the lab had been spending more time here.

It had its ups and downs. They were all scientists

who were at the top of their respective fields when they were active.

However, they hadn't been active in ten years.

All three partners funded this lab so the next generation could take over. They still loved to offer their input despite the advancements they didn't understand.

"Good morning." I tried to sound chipper, but troubled, when I entered their spacious office.

"Good morning Dr. Bellin. How are you faring?" Dr. Ketta Braithwaite, once the planet's most accomplished thermonuclear physicist, smiled warmly.

"It's difficult to say." I looked at my feet.

"The riot gave us all a fright," Dr. Urlough Hodgins gave me a look of genuine sympathy. He once dominated the interplanetary chemistry field.

"Yes, but that's not where I'm experiencing difficulties."

"Out with it, Doctor. We aren't getting any younger." Dr. Nebula Kroner tutted. She was a trailblazer in my field until she retired. Retirement didn't suit her. I got the sense she didn't like me very much.

"My bodyguard is detrimental to my work," I said in a rush. "I'd appreciate someone less disruptive or to not have a bodyguard at all."

"Out of the question," Dr. Hodgins frowned. "The

knowledge you're gathering is invaluable. You must be protected."

"I understand but surely the Puppet Master is more than capable of guarding me," I pointed out.

"Watch it," Dr. Kroner warned. "You're still green, Dr. Bellin. I could recommend someone with more experience for this job if I had the mind to.

Like herself, no doubt.

"Of course." I bowed my head. "My apologies. I'll make it work."

"Do that. You're dismissed." Dr. Kroner returned her attention to her console. I left the office silently.

Jalok was still talking with Eluna. I could see his discomfort from where I stood, and smothered a giggle.

He had been happy to flirt when he thought it made me upset. Now that someone was taking him up on it, he didn't seem to know what to do.

Goof.

Jalok hadn't seen me come out of the office. Without thinking twice, I hurried out of the lab.

I reached the market in less than five minutes.

"Hudd? Can I borrow your WindJet?"

"What for?" Hudd didn't look up from the eight-foot fish he was deboning.

"Work. I have really important data to collect and the riot hit the lab transportation units hard."

"You scratch it, you pay for it."

"Thanks, Hudd! You're the best." I hurried around back but not before I saw a smile from beneath Hudd's beard.

The WindJet was a single person hovercraft, like my bike only better in every way. I turned it on and kicked it into high gear. I was out of Kaster in moments.

The WindJet wasn't the speediest of transport units. It took some time for me to reach the *Vengeance* crater. I parked the WindJet besides the opening of the tunnel and hurried inside.

I touched the first vine I found.

"I wasn't expecting you today." The Puppet Master's voice in my mind was so comforting. I didn't realize until now how much I'd missed my friend.

"It wasn't easy getting here," I admitted. "But I'm anxious to continue the work we started last time we spoke."

"No more experiments in the jungle," the Puppet Master warned me.

"I promise!" I lifted my free hand in defense. "Did the neuro-monitors I left hooked up continue to record?"

"They did."

"Excellent! They've been collecting data this whole time!"

I hurried down the tunnel to the mini lab I'd left

behind. Everything was just as I left it. I sent the new data back to my lab.

"I'm getting close to something, I know it. If I can just break this down into something we can understand and replicate, we can do amazing things."

I hunkered down in my usual spot with my back against one of the Puppet Master's vines. He told me about riots that had been happening in other smaller cities but not even he predicted the one in Kaster.

"Kaster is my favorite city out of all the ones you humans have constructed."

"Really?" I grinned.

"It keeps itself balanced with the resources available to it."

A memory from a previous conversation suddenly resurfaced in my mind.

"Did the Ancient Enemies ever try to leech your lifeforce from this planet?"

"If they tried, you wouldn't be here now to ask me," the Puppet Master answered.

"What are the Ancient Enemies?" A voice from behind me startled me to my feet. Jalok stood in the tunnel, weapons drawn.

He looked furious.

Uh oh.

"What the hell are you doing here?" I snapped.

"I should ask you the same thing."

"I informed the proper authorities that you were here alone," the Puppet Master admitted.

"What?" I shouted.

"What, what?" Jalok snapped back. He wasn't touching the Puppet Master. He couldn't hear the voice.

"Be quiet," I told him. "This is the first chance I've gotten to continue our work. Why would you try to take that away?" I asked the Puppet Master.

"Your safety is important to me. You are my friend."

I couldn't help but feel touched by the Puppet Master's concerns, even as I was annoyed by the results. I ran a hand along one of the vines.

"Are you talking to it?"

"Yes, I talk to him frequently. It's part of my job and my favorite part of the day."

"Have fun." Jalok plopped down on the ground and made himself comfortable.

"Get up." I kicked at his boot. "If we're stuck together, you're going to make yourself useful."

"This will be most amusing," the Puppet Master chuckled.

JALOK

"I think we can call it a day." Wiping the sweat off her brow, Dottie looked at one of her screens and nodded to herself. Her hair was slightly disheveled, and slight lines of exhaustion were starting to show around her eyes.

Still, she seemed to be brimming with energy all the same.

"You think?" I asked her. We had spent the entire day holed up in the cavern, and my datapad told me that the sun had already set outside. "We should've been back in Kaster by now. This is a breach of security protocol. To travel by night is—"

"You're my bodyguard, right?" She cut me short, both hands on her hips.

Blowing a stray lock of hair away from her face, she

waited for me to say something. I just frowned, so she pressed on.

"It's your job to protect me so that I can do my job."

"That's right."

"Well, I'm doing my job," she smiled, her perfect white teeth peeking from between her lips. "As long as you do yours, we'll be fine." I shook my head. She was making it harder for me to do my job, but it was useless to tell her that.

She already knew, and she didn't care.

"Let's just get going," I told her, watching as she packed her instruments. A few of them she left on the worktable she had set up in the cavern, but others she packed inside a metallic briefcase.

The cavern was really nothing more than a wide space where a number of tunnels intersected. Nothing like the main chamber where the Puppet Master's heart? Body? Whatever lived.

Before she turned to leave, she went down on one knee and caressed one of the vines, her fingertips softly running down its length.

I could hear her whisper but, even though I couldn't make out the words, I knew she was talking with the Puppet Master.

Dottie acted with zealous professionalism around me at all times, but the way she talked to the Puppet Master suggested more than a professional relationship. Somehow, she had become friends with one of the most powerful—if not the most powerful—beings on the planet.

And maybe I was feeling just a touch jealous of that.

"Alright, I'm ready." Standing up, she wiped the dust off her hands against her trousers. Smiling, she pressed her briefcase against my chest and started walking out of the cavern. I looked down at the briefcase and pursed my lips.

I was her bodyguard, not her mule.

"Wait for me," I grumbled, hurrying after her as the briefcase dangled from my left hand. She just threw me an amused glance, looking back at me over her shoulder, and kept on walking at the exact same pace.

Outside, the baby-blue of an afternoon sky had been replaced by a dark canvas, thousands of tiny stars dotting the night.

The comfortable warmth had also given way to a chilly breeze, and I felt some relief as I thought of the hovercraft I had borrowed from the motor pool.

Since most regular transport units had been in use when Dottie disappeared, I had to borrow one of the hovercrafts meant for diplomatic missions. That meant heated-seats, a noiseless engine, and engines that could put us in Kaster in half the time a regular transport shuttle could manage.

All in all, things could be worse.

"That's fancy," Dottie whistled as she found the hovercraft. "You sure know how to travel in style, Jalok."

"I didn't choose it," I merely said. "Now get in and let's get out of here."

"I'm not leaving in that." Turning on her heels to face, she threw me a glance that I knew meant trouble. "I came here in a WindJet." With that, she pointed beyond the diplomatic hovercraft. Right by the entrance of the tunnel sat a single-person transport unit.

WindJets were popular in Kaster, as they offered people the most bang for their buck, but they were subpar transport units.

"I don't care. You're leaving in *that*." I pointed toward my hovercraft. No way was Dottie driving that WindJet piece of crap back to Kaster. She'd freeze herself to death. "I'll send someone to pick that up in the morning."

"That's not happening," she said, slightly narrowing her eyes. "I borrowed it from a friend, and I'm not leaving it out here."

"I don't care what—"

"I'm not leaving it out there," she repeated, crossing her arms over her chest. She stared at me, almost as if she was daring me to do something about it. Gritting my teeth, I glanced at the WindJet and tried to measure it. The damn thing was too large for me to fit inside my hovercraft.

"Fine," I said through gritted teeth. "You take the hovercraft, and I'll drive that damn thing back."

"Are you sure?" She arched one eyebrow, a suspicious expression on her face. "It's going to be a cold ride, you know?"

"That's exactly why I'll take it," I said. "I have to keep you safe. Now get inside the damn hovercraft."

Reaching inside one of her pockets, she grabbed a set of keys and threw them toward me. I caught them mid-air and, without saying a word, went toward the WindJet.

"Enjoy," she laughed as she climbed aboard the hovercraft, sounding more enthusiastic about the whole thing than she should.

"I'll drive in front of you to set the pace," I told her as I climbed onto the WindJet. It was a clumsy thing, one size too small for me, and I wondered if the chassis wouldn't give under my weight.

I started the engine, holding my breath as it pushed itself off the ground, and placed both hands on the handle.

Engaging the thrusters, I started heading toward the hovercraft when a cloud of dust hit me like a brick.

Dottie had pushed the hovercraft off the ground

hastily, and it looked like she had no intention of allowing me to set the pace.

When the dust finally settled around me, the hovercraft's tail lights were nothing but a faint speck of light in the distance.

"That damned woman," I growled, pushing the WindJet to its absolute limits. The metal creaked as the engines worked up a frenzy, and I could almost feel the bolts in the chassis rattling in place.

I was going as fast as I could, and it was absolutely useless. It was impossible to catch up to Dottie. Cursing under my breath, the cold biting into my skin, I clenched my jaw and braced myself for the long journey ahead.

By the time I arrived in Kaster, the city was already in a deep slumber. The traffic was almost non-existent, and the WindJet howled through the streets almost as angrily as I felt.

When I got to Dottie's apartment building, the hovercraft was neatly tucked in a vacant parking spot. I pulled up next to it and, after climbing down from the WindJet, I inspected it for any scratches. I would have my ass chewed if I returned a diplomatic transport unit with a dent.

"At least that went well," I muttered once I was sure that the only problem with the hovercraft was the thin layer of dust that covered it. Pushing the WindJet's keys into one pocket, I stepped inside the building and climbed the stairs until I stood in front of Dottie's apartment door.

I banged my fist against it, and from the adjoining apartment came a tirade of threats from an elderly voice.

"What the hell do you think you're doing?" Dottie asked me as she got the door. "Come in. You're gonna wake up the entire building."

"You shouldn't have ran away," I told her, ignoring her annoyed stare.

"I didn't run away," she protested. "You told me to take the hovercraft, and that's exactly what I did."

"I also told her I'd set the pace."

"I must've missed that part," she said, a devious glint in her eyes. She was enjoying this. "Well, now that you've checked up on me and seen that I'm safe, you're free to go."

"What are you talking about?"

"It's late and I still haven't gotten dinner," she sighed, and her enjoyment was slowly being replaced by frustration. "Go home and let me rest. We'll see each other in the morning, alright? I promise I won't run away."

"I don't think you understand."

"Understand what?"

"I'm in charge of your protection," I said and, as she

narrowed her eyes into slits, I realized I would have to spell it out for her. "This is a round-the-clock job."

"You've gotta be kidding," she breathed out, raking one hand over her face. "You're telling me you're going to sleep here? In my apartment?"

"I can arrange for you to spend the night at a government's facility, if that's more to your liking."

"Alright, fine," she muttered, already turning away from me. She went across the apartment, disappeared into the bedroom, and returned a couple of seconds later with a pillow and blanket.

She threw them on top of the battered old couch in her living room, almost as if she was getting rid of a pile of rubble, and then pointed toward it all. "You can sleep here."

"Thank you." I wasn't looking forward to spending the night here, but I figured it wouldn't hurt to be polite.

Maybe that would mellow Dottie out.

She just rolled her eyes at me, one of those annoying things human insisted on doing, and went towards the ensuite kitchen. She was rummaging through her fridge when someone knocked at the door.

Dottie tensed up immediately. I hated the wave of fear that had swept that confident woman away. Instead of saying anything, I just gave her a little smile.

"I got it." Pushing myself off the couch, I got the

door and greeted the delivery man standing there. He pushed a couple of bags into my hands, and the smell of greasy take-away immediately took over Dottie's little apartment.

"You're kidding."

"I ordered dinner for us on my way here," I told her, pleased with the fact that this time I was the one surprising her.

Setting the bags on the kitchen counter, I started removing the little plastic containers from the inside. Frowning, she perched herself on the stools lining the counter, right beside me. I didn't wait for her as I dove in the food. After spending the whole day holed up in a cave in the middle of nowhere, I was ravenous.

We ate in silence, and that suited me just fine.

"You're not very talkative, are you?" Dottie finally said, her voice cutting through the silence.

"Don't have much to talk about with you."

"You must be a lot of fun."

"Sometimes."

"You're impossible," she sighed, rolling her eyes again. "You're one of those military guys that doesn't have a life, aren't you?"

"I guess you could say that." I wasn't feeling particularly inclined to share my life story with her, and I hoped my vague answers were enough to silence her.

They weren't, of course. Dottie's curiosity seemed to know no bounds.

I wondered how the Puppet Master could deal with all her questions without going insane.

"There must be something you like doing outside your job," she insisted, and I finally raised my eyes from the food. "C'mon, give me something. If you're going to stay here, it's only fair I get to know you."

"It's just like you said," I shrugged. "The military's my life."

"That's so interesting." She was being sarcastic, and her eyes rolled once more. If she kept on doing that, I wouldn't be too surprised if they popped out of her sockets.

"Fine," I relented. I would have to give her something or she would never shut up. "I grew up in a military family. My grandfather fought in the Uther wars, and my father was part of the assault on Azan's moons. He was in charge of a Skotan squad, and he was part of the first wave landing there, right behind enemy lines."

She looked at me with a surprised expression, and I could tell she had no idea what I was talking about. I didn't care. "I studied in a military school, and I put a lot of sweat and blood into it. The training is rigorous, and only a few make it."

"But you graduated."

"Yes," I nodded, and felt my heart tighten as I remembered graduation day. The smoke billowing out from crumbling buildings, the screams of agony, and the explosions. "The Xathi attacked on the first day I donned my uniform. My father, a battle hardened veteran, died that day. I've been fighting ever since."

I held her gaze for a moment, but then looked away. I had no idea why I had told her all this. I tried to avoid remembering that day whenever I could, but here I was now...spilling my guts to a tiny little human woman just because she was pretty.

"I had no idea," she whispered softly. Climbing down from her stool, she turned to me and wrapped her delicate arms around my torso.

And my brain short circuited.

"What are you doing?"

"It's a hug, you idiot," she snapped at me. "Just roll with it."

Hesitantly, I put my arms around her, her tiny frame so frail against my chest that I was almost afraid of hurting her. Her scent was like a drug, something I never even knew existed, and now would kill to keep a steady supply of it.

"You're not so bad, are you?" She whispered, her voice smooth and tender. Then, before I could do anything about it, she went on tiptoes and kissed my cheek. I looked straight into her eyes as she pulled back, so surprised that I didn't even know how to react.

Her lips were slightly parted, and there was something about her that was short-circuiting my brain. My mind became like a hollow cavern, not a single thought floating in there.

She smiled then.

Going on her tiptoes again, she looked as if she was about to kiss my forehead. I moved down so that she could do it, but I did it in such an awkward way that my mouth crashed against hers.

The touch of her lips was electric, and my heart rate shot up in an instant.

It was an accident, and yet...we took our time before pulling back.

Clearing her throat, her cheeks turning red, she looked down at her feet. "I think I'm gonna hit the bed right now." She padded her way to the bedroom but, before stepping inside, she looked back at me over her shoulder. "Have a good night, Jalok."

"You too, Dottie."

It was hard to fall asleep that night, and the couch had little to do with it.

DOTTIE

I tiptoed out of my room the next morning. Jalok was asleep on the couch. He was so broad and tall that not all of his body could fit on the couch at one time. The blanket I'd loaned him looked like a doily now.

I felt guilty for not giving up the bed for him.

But only a little.

I moved silently around him, avoiding all the spots in the floor I knew to be creaky. I can't believe we kissed last night. Kind of. Honestly, I wasn't sure what that was.

Jalok made my blood boil. I wanted nothing more than to be rid of him forever and never think of him again. Yet, I enjoyed talking to him last night.

And when we touched... something in my brain

must have just turned off. I couldn't explain it any other way.

He was still the aggressive rage-titan I'd met during the riots, but now I understood his rage a little better.

It must be horrible for him to be stuck here when he wanted to fight where he felt like he could make a difference.

He must feel the way I felt yesterday when I wasn't allowed to work with the Puppet Master.

Restless. Irritable. Short tempered.

I crept into my kitchen and slowly opened my refrigeration unit. It was empty save for two end pieces of bread I'd been avoiding, a tin of leftover noodles and an empty carton of orange juice I'd forgotten to throw away.

I didn't spend much time in my kitchen. I either ate at the lab cafeteria or picked up something in the market.

The fishermen of Kaster worked hard. I liked supporting them, and it made everything easier for me.

Jalok took care of dinner last night. I was hoping to take care of breakfast to return the favor but it looked like I'd have to go out and grab something unless he wanted to eat noodles on a toasted end piece of bread.

Not even I wanted to eat that.

"What time is it?" A groggy voice came from the couch.

"A little after seven," I guessed by the way the light came in. "How'd you sleep?"

"I'm bigger than your couch," Jalok laughed. "How do you think I slept?"

"I'm sorry. I should've offered my bed."

"I've slept in far more uncomfortable places. Though, you really ought to get a new couch."

"I'll put that on the list," I snorted.

Jalok stood up from the couch to fold the blanket I'd lent him. At some point, after I'd retired to my room, he'd removed his shirt. I found myself unable to look away from his broad shoulders. His muscles worked as he arranged the blanket in a neat square and set it on the back of the couch.

Our eyes locked when he turned around to face me.

"Is something the matter?" He asked.

"I, uh," I scrambled to come up with something to say. "I wanted to thank you for telling me what you told me last night. You seem a little more human to me now."

"There's no need to insult me," he teased.

"Very funny." I rolled my eyes. "Seriously, thanks. I feel like I should tell you something personal too. I don't want you to have an advantage over me."

"Militaristically speaking, you hold the advantage over me. You could use the personal information I divulged last night for leverage."

"You're a dedicated soldier at heart. Give me all your money before I tell everyone."

"You're horrible at using information for leverage," he laughed.

"I take pride in not knowing how to blackmail someone."

"You really think I'm dedicated?" Jalok tilted his head to one side.

"I do. You remind me of my brother actually."

Jalok took a seat on the couch and gestured to the empty space next to him.

I nudged his shoulder as I took a seat. The whole couch smelled like him. Warm, spicy. Intriguing.

"Ankou doesn't have a formal military," I began.

"I've noticed."

"Aside from the city guards that handle petty crimes, there's a Search and Rescue team that has divisions in every city. For as long as I can remember, that's all my brother wanted to do. He had all these crazy dreams about rushing into burning buildings or throwing himself into ravines to save people. He worked really hard to earn his spot even though he had to leave Kaster to keep it."

"Where did he end up?"

"Fraga, the only city smaller than Kaster. I didn't think he should go. It was insulting to send him to such a small place. Of course, I kept that thought to myself. He didn't need his little sister ruining his happiness."

I lightly raked my nails over my wrist. It was an anxious habit of mine that I'd never managed to shake.

"I shouldn't have held back. I should've told him what I thought about Fraga. I knew he wouldn't be happy there even if he was on the Search and Rescue team."

"He wasn't happy?"

"No. Nothing bad happened in Fraga, ever. Mayor Vidia was on top of local crime. The economy of the little city was booming. Everyone was content. Every once in a while, my brother would get called to help someone find their keys or their car. One time he had to perform the Heimlich maneuver on an elderly woman who choked on her food one table over from where he was having lunch."

"That sounds horrible," Jalok frowned.

"It was for him. He never complained. Not once. Even if he wasn't happy about it, he swore to do his duty. He was so sure that once the higher-ups saw how dedicated he was, they'd move him somewhere where he could do some real good. He rationalized that his time in Fraga was some kind of test."

"Was it?"

"My brother served on Search and Rescue in Fraga for three years. Not once did any higher up ever recognize his efforts. After the first year, things started to take a toll on him. His messages were shorter and fewer. I once went three months without hearing from him. I wanted to go visit him but he always told me to stay in Kaster and finish my schooling."

"He probably wanted to spare you from seeing how far he'd fallen," Jalok said softly. I bit my bottom lip and nodded.

"Is he still in Fraga now?"

This was the hard part.

"I don't know," I whispered. "When the Xathi attacked Fraga, they destroyed almost everything. The lists of the dead and the missing are still incomplete but I haven't heard from him since before the attack."

"I'm so sorry to hear that." Jalok reached for my hand and pulled it away from my wrist. The area I'd been absentmindedly scratching looked red and angry. I took my hand from his and placed it flat on my lap.

"I don't talk about it often." My throat felt thick and clogged. Words didn't come easily.

"Understandable. We don't have to talk about it anymore. Thanks for telling me. I promise not to use this against you for leverage."

Despite everything, I laughed.

"Thanks."

I blinked away the tears that started to build up behind my lids.

"Are you hungry?" I asked in an unnaturally perky voice. Jalok didn't comment on the forced cheerfulness.

"Skotans are always hungry," he grinned.

"Great. I have no food in my refrigerator. We'll have to go to the market."

"Don't you have to be at the lab?"

"The whole city takes the day off today. It's when the fishermen bring in the best catches of the week. Like clockwork. It means the market is going to be crazy busy."

"Not a problem. I can part a crowd," Jalok smirked.

"Give me a minute to get dressed and we'll go."

Once in my room, I opened my closet and sighed. All of the clothing I owned was practical for either lab work or field work. I didn't have anything a normal person would consider pretty.

Not that I wanted to be pretty.

Why would I want to be pretty?

Ridiculous.

I was just going to the market. A linen shirt and denim pants would be just fine. Still, owning a flowy, floral dress wouldn't kill me. Maybe Alinda the seamstress would have one at her stall today.

Jalok stood in the kitchen with his head in the refrigerator when I came out of my room.

"Trying to cool that hot head of yours?" I joked.

"Trying to figure out how you derive all necessary nutrients from the contents of your chilling unit."

"I eat out a lot," I explained. "Let's go before all the good fish are gone."

I grabbed him by the forearm and pulled him out the door.

The market square was bustling by the time we arrived. Just about every citizen of Kaster was out and about today.

"Why didn't the rioters pick today to act?" Jalok wondered.

"I bet the brains of that operation wasn't from here. Don't you love this?" I gestured to the shouting, jostling, laughing crowd as everyone bartered for goods.

"It's chaotic," Jalok said. "Part of my job description his to make order from chaos."

"That's awfully vague and poetic for a soldiers job description."

"I took some creative liberties," Jalok shrugged. "How do people avoid getting robbed?"

"No one here would rob anyone," I scoffed. "I could go up to anyone and ask for a few credits and they'd oblige. This is a community built on trust and friendship."

"Must be nice." Jalok's smile didn't hold any trace of sarcasm.

"Dottie!" I turned to see Hudd calling me. I hurried over with Jalok in tow.

"Hey, Hudd. How's the haul? I'll bring back the WindJet when there's not quite such a crush."

"Excellent. I saved you some of the best specimens."

Hudd led me over to a small ice chest teeming with glittering fish.

"You didn't have to do that," I grinned. "I'll take the three little ones. Can you wrap them?"

"Of course."

I started to move away from Hudd when he gently grabbed my arm.

"I wanted to warn you that a few marketgoers are staring at you and your companion," he murmured. "Normally, I wouldn't think much of it but since that riot..." he trailed off.

"Thanks for the heads up."

As I waited for my fish, I casually looked around the market. Sure enough, a few people were giving Jalok and me odd looks. Knowing none of them would dare try anything with Jalok nearby, I elected to ignore them.

What else could I do?

"Hold these." I dumped the wrapped fish into Jalok's arms. "We have a lot more to buy."

"Dottie?" Jalok called after me. I turned back to look at him.

"Yeah?"

"What's your brother's name?"

"What?" I blinked in confusion. Why did he want to know?

"Your brother. What's his name?" Jalok asked again.

"Adam."

JALOK

"Give me a moment," I said and, before Dottie could reply, I started moving back.

I kept my eyes on her as I stepped into a side alley and, once I was happy she wouldn't move out of sight, I grabbed my comms unit from my belt.

I waited as I got dialed into Nyheim's system, Rokul's ID number flashing on the little screen, and a couple of seconds later his voice boomed through the intercom. "Jalok? Is something wrong?" He asked, his tone showing more concern that I was expecting.

"No," I hurried to say. "I just wanted to ask you for a favor."

"A favor?" His voice came slightly garbled through the static, but I could still notice the surprise in his voice. "What's this about? You're not the kind of guy to go around asking for favors. Are you in trouble?"

"No, I'm fine," I repeated. "Do you know the woman I've been assigned to? Dottie?"

"I've heard of her. Some scientist, right? I heard she's working on the Puppet Master."

"She's working *with* the Puppet Master," I corrected him.

Dottie had frowned and wagged her finger at me after I had made the same mistake as Rokul's, and it seemed like that had stuck with me. "But never mind that. I just wanted you to take a quick look at her file."

"Her file, huh? What's this about? If you're interested in her, I suggest you ask her out for dinner or something. A way to a woman's heart isn't exactly through her private files."

"Seems like you're quite the expert," I grumbled. "It's nothing like that. Can you pull her file or not?"

"Fine, fine," he said, and seconds later I heard the mechanical clacking of a keyboard. "Right, I have it in front of me. What do you want to know?"

"She has a brother, right?"

"Yes, the name's Adam," he replied. "He was part of a Search and Rescue unit in Fraga."

"Is there nothing else?"

"Not really. What's this about?"

"Apparently her brother disappeared after the attacks on Fraga. She hasn't heard from him ever since."

"Oh, I see what you're doing."

"I'm not doing anything," I said, trying to sound as resolute as I could. "Can you just dig into this and see what kind of intel you can find?"

"Sure can. I don't know how much information I'll find, though. Most of the records were destroyed during the invasion, and I know some field units have started using pen and paper to update their case files. Can you believe that? It's madness, if you ask me. The tech guys have been working day and night to get the databases up and running, and those idiots on the streets are making it all so—"

"Just let me know if you find something, alright?"

"Alright, I got you, Don Juan."

"What?"

"Don Juan," he repeated. There was a slight pause, and then I heard him sigh. "Never mind that. It's just something women call guys like you."

"Guys like me? What's that supposed to mean?"

"Nothing, really," he said, and I knew I wouldn't get a straight answer out of him. Not that it mattered, anyway. "I'll keep you updated, Jalok. Be safe."

"Thank you." Clicking the comms unit off, I strapped it to my belt again.

Dottie remained in front of the same stall, chatting

it up with the vendor, and I slowly made my way through the crowd and toward her.

I wasn't really sure on why I had decided to help her find her brother, but it didn't really matter.

Finding him would be tough and, even though I trusted Rokul to make the impossible happen, I didn't have high hopes.

"Where were you?" Dottie asked me as I closed in on her, a couple of bags hanging from her hands. "I thought you never left your post."

"I wasn't that far," I replied. "I was just giving a quick update on our status."

"Did you tell them I bought some fish and vegetables?" She threw me a smirk. "Do you want to have a bite before I cook them? They might be poisoned."

"That's not funny."

"That's because you don't have a sense of humor," she continued, and her smirk slowly turned into a smile. "Now hold this."

Without waiting for me to say something, she pushed her bags into my hands and strolled down the market.

Sighing, I followed after her, watching as she haggled with the vendors. For someone that looked so delicate, she sure knew how to handle herself.

She verbally wrestled with the vendors at every stall,

somehow buying her groceries for less credits than I would've thought possible, and it didn't take long before I looked like one scarecrows that dotted the fields outside Kaster, dozens of bangs hanging from my forearms.

"Is this going to take much longer?" I asked her, already growing impatient.

"No, I'm done," she smiled. "Let's just drop these things at the apartment. I want to take a quick shower, but then we can head to the lab."

We made our way through the market at a leisurely pace. Dottie didn't seem too concerned with getting to the lab on time, and I felt she was only going there to punch the clock. Her real work happened in that dimly-lit cavern, and I suspected she saw her time in the city lab as nothing but a necessary evil.

Once we were back in her apartment, I placed the bags on top of the kitchen counter. Dottie would've never been able to carry all the bags by herself, and I was pretty sure that she was taking advantage of me.

I didn't really mind it. As annoying as I had initially found this assignment, I was slowly starting to enjoy being around her.

"I won't take long," she said as she walked inside the bathroom and, just a couple of seconds later, I heard the sound of running water.

I sat on her old couch, the springs complaining as

they took my weight, but I quickly found myself up on my feet again.

From the inside the bathroom came Dottie's shrill voice, and I rushed out of the living room as fast as I could.

I pushed the door open fast and, with one hand resting on the butt of my weapon, I stepped inside Dottie's bathroom. She was standing under the running water of the shower and, before I could see anything but the vagueness of her silhouette, she grabbed the curtains and covered herself.

"What the hell are you doing here?" She cried out, her eyes shooting daggers at me. "Get out, you maniac!"

"You were screaming."

"Because the damn water has gone cold again," she said. "The plumbing in this building has lots of issues. There's no murderer hiding behind the toilet, but you can check if you want."

"And how the hell was I supposed to know all that?" Shaking my head, I was about to leave the bathroom when she cried out once more.

From the corner of my eye I saw her grabbing at the curtains, and her body went out of balance in a flash. She had slipped on the slick tile, but before she could fall on her head, I closed the distance between us and held her up.

She fell on my arms, the wet shower curtain

wrapped around her body, and I felt my heart kicking against my ribcage as I looked down at her. Her wet hair was plastered to her face, and tiny droplets of water ran down her rosy cheeks.

The flimsy curtain stuck to her body, showing me almost every single detail of her naked figure, and that was enough for a comfortable heat to spread all over my body.

My eyes landed on her slightly parted lips, and I felt that now familiar hollowness inside my mind. Before I even knew what the hell I was doing, I leaned into her.

Our lips touched, hesitant and eager at the same time, and I was about to pull back when she threw one arm around my neck. Pulling me into her, she parted my lips with her tongue and kissed me in a way I had never experienced before.

Our tongues danced in frenzied lust, and I ran one hand down the side of her body, that damned curtain the only barrier between us.

I felt her breasts pressed against my chest, her nipples hardening with each passing second, and that heat inside my body turned into a raging inferno.

I grew hard then, every fiber of my being desperate for her body, and I had to use all of my will power to stop myself from yanking the curtain back.

Keep it together, Jalok, I shouted inwardly.

Somehow, I pulled my lips from hers and helped her

to her feet. For a moment, none of us said a thing, the only sound that of the running water.

"I...I'll be out in a minute," she said. "I'll finish showering in an instant."

Clearing my throat, I found that I couldn't look into her eyes.

"I'll be waiting outside," I said and, with that, left the bathroom and closed the door behind me.

Inside my chest, my heart felt like a hand grenade.

What the hell had just happened?

DOTTIE

Jalok chuckled as I breezed past him standing in my living room and went out the door. I was anxious to get back to work. Most people dreaded going back on their days off but not me.

It had nothing to do with that kiss in the bathroom. Nothing.

I was especially excited because now that Jalok and I had broken the ice, so to speak, he'd probably agree to let me go see the Puppet Master.

The lab bosses still didn't want me to leave the premises for work but I believed that had more to do with Dr. Kroner's insecurities than my safety.

"What's the plan for today?" Jalok jogged to catch up to me once we were on the street.

"I've been called into a meeting as soon as we get to the

lab," I explained. "You're probably allowed to come in with me unless you want to take the time to flirt with Eluna."

"Will it piss you off if I do?"

"Not really," I shrugged.

But it did bother me. Just a tiny bit.

"Where's the fun in that then?"

I rolled my eyes and muffled a laugh.

"I have half a mind to make you talk to her just for that."

"She's likely more entertaining than a meeting anyway," Jalok agreed.

When we entered the lab, Jalok made his way to where Eluna sat. She did her best to pretend not to notice him as he approached.

I entered the spacious office of the lab founders.

"We've received an interesting message from the lab in Nyhiem," Dr. Braithwaite said with a smile.

"Is everything all right with the data I sent over?" My brow furrowed.

"The lab techs there are more than satisfied," Dr. Hodgins reported. "So, satisfied that they've sent over a request. A Dr. DeWitt would like an organic sample from the Puppet Master."

"Nyhiem has plenty of organic samples," I frowned.

"They want blood." Dr. Kroner clarified.

I blinked.

"I'm not sure that the Puppet Master has blood. He might have sap," I offered.

Dr. Kroner pushed a datapad in my direction.

"Read for yourself."

I picked up the datapad and scrolled through Dr. DeWitt's notes. I noticed that the notes in question had not been sent over to my person console.

I went ahead and forwarded them to myself.

"I'll go talk to the Puppet Master. If anyone knows whether or not he has blood, it's him."

I set the datapad back down.

Dr. Kroner's eyes flickered to the screen. From where she sat, she could see that I'd sent the notes to myself. Her thin lips pursed but she didn't' say anything.

"Take your bodyguard," Dr. Braithwaite said.

"Of course," I nodded. "Is that all?"

"You're dismissed." Dr. Kroner said curtly.

I left the office and walked over to where Jalok stood talking to Eluna.

"Good news, we're going on a field trip." I clapped him on the shoulder.

Jalok turned away from his conversation with a grin.

"Good news, indeed. Where are we going?"

"Back to the crater. Do you have anything in that

fancy base camp of yours that can transport two people?"

"Certainly. The real question is, do you trust me to pilot it?"

"Absolutely not," I snorted. "The better question is, do I have a choice?"

"Nope! Let me call the camp and see what I can scrounge up."

Jalok stepped away to bark questions into his radio. Eluna gave me a strange smile.

"What?"

"You two hated each other a few days ago. What changed?"

"I don't know what you mean." I squared my shoulders, suddenly feeling defensive.

"You're practically best friends now."

"Don't be ridiculous. We've simply come to a mutual agreement that getting along is more conducive to a productive work environment."

"That's not a sentence a normal human would ever say," Eluna laughed. "Say whatever you want, but you two like each other."

"We don't even know each other."

"I've got a ride." Jalok jogged back over to us. He looked between me and Eluna. "Did I miss something."

"Nothing," Eluna grinned. "You two have fun collecting monster goop."

"I'm sure the Puppet Master appreciates the moniker," I laughed, grateful to Eluna for changing the subject.

At Jalok's base camp, a two-person aerial unit was ready and waiting for us.

"Don't crash it like you did last time." A K'ver gave Jalok a stern look.

"What is he talking about?" I gave Jalok a pointed look.

"Nothing. Sk'lar, you've become quite the jokester since entering a relationship with Phryne."

"I mean it, Jalok. We can't afford replacements."

"Yes, sir."

Jalok took my arm and helped me into the deep, narrow back seat of the aerial unit before climbing into the pilot's chair.

"So, what's the plan here?" Jalok called back once we were safely in the air. I pulled out my datapad that was synced to my console back at the lab.

"Looks like Dr. DeWitt has developed a theoretical serum to make hostile plant life more docile," I shouted over the roar of the aerial unit. "She thinks blood, or a similar substance, from the Puppet Master might provide some of the missing pieces."

"Is it really as simple as that?" Jalok looked over his shoulder at me.

"Eyes front, mister. Your bad piloting skills are not going to be what kills me."

"Answer my question. Don't you want me to learn new things? Isn't that the goal of a scientist?"

"You know nothing of my goals. No, it's not as simple as that I just wanted to put it into terms you could understand."

Jalok made a less than graceful landing in the center of the crater. I scrambled out of the aerial unit as quickly as I could without falling face first into the dirt.

"Aren't you trained for this kind of thing?"

"I'm trained for combat. I'm not a pilot," Jalok said in his defense.

The ground around us shifted as the Puppet Master's vines approached the aerial unit from underground.

"Look, you've got him all concerned with your graceless landing." I gestured toward the ground as a verdant tendril poked up above the earth. I laid a finger along it.

"Don't worry. Everything's fine." I told the Puppet Master. I felt his presence in my mind. Something felt off but I couldn't place it.

"I would have assumed your companion received more rigorous training with that apparatus."

"That's what I said," I chuckled and removed my hand from the tendril. It slunk back underground.

"Talking about me when I can't listen isn't very nice." Jalok chided.

"The Puppet Master was just making sure I'm okay," I explained.

"How did you get so close to it?" Jalok asked as we walked across the crater to the tunnel.

"Talking with him. Spending time with him. You know, the usual activities that form a friendship."

Jalok pushed back a cluster of dead roots so I wouldn't have to duck when entering the tunnel. When we arrived at my makeshift lab, he took a moment to look around.

"You always leave your stuff lying around like this?"

"It's out of sight," I reasoned. "Your teams know not to mess with it. If a radical or scavenger come across it, the Puppet Master will stop them from messing with it. It's easier than lugging everything back and forth. Plus, if I keep my monitors running overnight, I get even more data."

"What kind of data are you after?" Jalok asked.

"What's with the sudden interest?" I asked with a small smile.

"Can't a Skotan be a soldier and curious about science?"

"Fair point. I'm measuring the Puppet Master's flow of energy, for lack of better term. Once understand how he can make things grow, we can replicate it. It'll be a big step in solving the food crisis."

"That's actually very impressive," Jalok smiled.

"Thank you for the validation," I teased. "Put your hand on the Puppet Master if you want to be part of the next conversation."

"Is it going to be science jargon I won't understand?"

"Maybe." I snorted before placing my palm against the thickest vine close to me. Jalok followed suit.

"*What brings you here today?*" The Puppet Master asked.

"Oh, that's unsettling." Jalok's hand went to his forehead.

"First time?" I asked.

"*I have not felt this one's presence before,*" the Puppet Master answered.

"What he said." Jalok jerked his head at the vines.

"You'll get used to it," I assured Jalok before returning to the reason I'd come here. "I have an unusual request."

"*I'm listening,*" the Puppet Master said.

"A colleague out of Nyhiem believes she's on the verge of discovery. She's asked me to retrieve something from you to further her studies."

"Why didn't this colleague come herself?" Jalok asked, interrupting our conversation.

"Because he likes me better," I jested.

Jalok gave me an odd smile and shook his head.

"I have a stronger relationship with you than almost any of the others that study me," the Puppet Master confirmed. *"What do you need?"*

"Do you have blood?" I blurted.

"I do not."

"What's the closest thing you have to blood?"

"I believe you humans would compare it to sap. It isn't truly any form of sap, although it does provide nourishment. There simply is not a word in your lexicon that would describe it otherwise." the Puppet Master supplied.

"Are you all right with me taking a sample?"

"Of course."

The Puppet Master lifted another tendril for me to take a sample from. I gathered my tools for sample collection.

"Is everything all right?" I asked when my hands made contact with the Puppet Master again. Jalok gave me a quizzical look and knelt down beside me. He placed his hand on the Puppet Master near my own.

"I suppose I cannot hide my troubles when our consciousness' are linked," the Puppet Master replied.

"You can tell me if something's bothering you. We're friends after all, even if I do run the occasional experiment on you."

"I can step away, if you'd like," Jalok offered.

"*That won't be necessary,*" the Puppet Master said. "*What I have to say pertains to you.*"

"What is it?" I pressed.

"*I felt a presence through the cosmos the other day,*" the Puppet Master explained. "*One I haven't felt in ages. It was a warning from one of my species. They must've used the last of their energy to contact me. Something was sapping their energy, their lifeforce.*"

"Does this have something to do with the Ancient Enemies you told me about?" I prompted.

"*I'm not sure. They never answered my signal back. But there's a possibility that the Ancient Enemies are involved.*"

JALOK

I tensed up as I heard the words 'ancient enemies.'

Fen hadn't known much about it, but her words had been ominous. That didn't surprise me. Intergalactic beings that seemed to have as their enemies something as powerful as the Puppet Master?

An ominous tone was to be expected.

"This signal you've received, how do you know it was a warning?" I said, not exactly sure on how to interact with the Puppet Master.

I had always seen Dottie say her words out loud but, somehow, I had the impression it could read my thoughts.

"*I believe you would call it a feeling,*" he explained, his disembodied voice almost dreamlike. I felt his words inside my head like tendrils, curling themselves around my own thoughts. The experience was unsettling. *"We don't communicate like you do."*

"That's not very helpful," I muttered.

"You are correct," the Puppet Master continued. *"Any other time, and their message would have a clearer meaning. But we have been growing weak. Dying, if you will. I might be the only one that's left of my kind."*

Its words remained neutral and steady, but I could still detect a note of sadness underneath all of it.

Maybe it was just my imagination. After all, I couldn't fathom how it'd feel to be the last one of my species.

"You said something was sapping their energy. Is that something the Ancient Enemies can do?"

"There are many things the Ancient Enemies can do." The Puppet Master's tone remained calm, and that was making the whole thing even more unsettling. How could it remain so calm when talking about such a thing?

"Alright, and what *exactly* do you know about them?" I insisted. "Fen mentioned doom and despair, but that doesn't tell us much. But she did mention that they were around even before the Urai had developed interstellar travel."

There was a slight pause, almost as if the Puppet Master was thinking.

"Doom and despair, yes," it finally said. *"The Urai would*

know of it, although their version of things might be different than mine. I was already awake even before the Urai called themselves by that name, and the Ancient Enemies were already a name that wise species wouldn't utter in the dark."

I wasn't liking any of this.

First it had been Fen, with her stories of unspoken terrors, and now even this omniscient vine creature seemed to fear those Ancient Assholes.

I thought of pressing the Puppet Master for more, but I knew I wouldn't get much out of it. He was being cagey about the whole thing.

"Is there anything else you can tell me about those Ancient Enemies?" I tried one last time, and the Puppet Master's was a curt one.

"Not much, but yes," it said, and then there was only silence. I took that as its polite way of saying that he'd say more, but not to me.

Knowing that all this was above my paygrade, I reached for the comms unit in my belt.

"What are you doing?" Dottie asked. Surprisingly, she had been silent as I talked with the Puppet Master.

"I'm contacting HQ. This stuff about the Ancient Enemies...it's worrying, and I think it's time the General starts focusing on it."

Dottie said nothing at that, but I could tell she wasn't exactly happy.

Whenever the General needed to work with the

Puppet Master, her scientific studies became a secondary priority.

Still, I hoped she would understand.

I was about to turn the comms unit on when a couple of vines gently wrapped themselves around my wrist. I jumped back, surprised, but the Puppet Master's soothing voice quickly made me relax. *"No need for that,"* it said. *"I can connect you directly to Sk'lar."*

"Alright," I said, not exactly sure on how to deal with the fact that the Puppet Master knew I intended to call Sk'lar.

Probably it could be useful, but it still creeped me out.

I waited as it worked its magic, and I felt as if my own thoughts were being pulled down a long narrow tunnel. I felt slightly dizzy and lightheaded, and then thoughts that weren't my own echoed in my mind.

"Jalok?" I heard Sk'lar's voice, as clear as if he was standing next to me. *"What in the—"*

"Just listen to me," I cut him short. I was slightly weirded out with this telepathic connection thing, and I didn't want it to last long. "I need you to get in touch with General Rouhr. It's urgent."

"The General? What's going on?"

"I...I'm not sure," I admitted. "But it concerns the Ancient Enemies. I think it'd be best if he came down here to the Puppet Master."

"Alright, I'll pass that message along," he said. *"But the General's out right now. It might take a couple of hours before he gets there."*

"I'll wait." As if guessing I intended to end the connection, the Puppet Master's vines finally let go of my wrist, gently brushing against my skin as they slid out. "Seems like we might be here for a while," I told Dottie, and she pursed her lips slightly.

"You're worried about the Ancient Enemies, aren't you?"

"Not exactly," I shrugged. "It's not my job to worry. But I think it's time for the General to start doing some worrying of his own."

"Right." The lines on her forehead deepened slightly, but then she just sighed audibly and shook her head.

Tucking a stray lock of hair over one ear, she then grabbed her instruments and returned to her tasks. I sat by a rock formation as I watched her work, and she spent the next couple of hours carefully collecting sap out of the vines.

As she worked, my eyes took in her figure in a manner that wasn't exactly professional.

I had tried to forget about that little moment inside her bathroom, but it was impossible to do so.

Her slender figure, her naked skin, and the warmth of her mouth...all those things were far too powerful for me to ignore. In fact, the more I tried to push them to a corner of my mind, the more they insisted on pushing their way to the front.

"Get a hold of yourself, Jalok."

"What was that?" Dottie asked, looking up from her instruments, that curiosity of hers making her eyes brighter. I looked back at her, not saying a word, and my heart started beating just a little bit faster. She was beautiful.

Clearing my throat, I looked away from her.

"It was nothing," I said. "Just thinking out loud."

"Didn't know you could think," she laughed, an amused smile on her lips as she teased me.

Before, I would've been annoyed at her sassiness, but now...it was almost endearing.

"I might be a brute, but I have a brain." Folding my arms over my chest, I locked my eyes on her.

She was about to say something when the sound of heavy footsteps started echoing throughout the tunnel. I laid one hand on my belt, ready to reach for my rifle, but relaxed as General Rouhr stepped from the shadows into the cavern.

"Jalok," he said, and I straightened my back and saluted him. "At ease."

"Did you come alone, General?"

"Sk'lar's waiting outside." Walking straight toward the large vine, he reached for it with his open hand, his fingers gently touching it. "I'm going to ask you to step outside for a moment."

"Very well, sir." Exchanging a quick glance with Dottie, I made a slight gesture that indicated for her to follow me. She looked at Rouhr, curious, but said nothing as she walked past him. "C'mon, let's give the General a little privacy."

"What exactly is going?" She whispered, laying her hands on my arm.

The hair on the back of my neck stood up on end as I felt her fingertips on my bicep, and I had to suck in a deep breath so that could regain my focus.

"The General's being cautious," I explained. "Just like the Puppet Master. You've probably noticed it by now, but your plant friend is pretty hesitant about sharing what he knows about those Ancient Enemies."

"I noticed, yes."

"Whatever information he has, he probably doesn't want it to spread. It would probably cause a panic, I figure."

Ahead of us, the bright light of a warm day cut into the darkness through the tunnel's mouth. "I'm sure that the General will let us know what's going on. He just needs to assess the intel firsthand before making a decision."

"I don't like all this secrecy," Dottie sighed. "That's

not how you should handle information. And, definitely, that's not how you should make a decision."

She made a slight pause then, and I could almost hear the gears turning inside her head. "But if the Puppet Master trusts the General...well, I guess these two know what they're doing."

"We're talking about a battle-hardened General and an overpowered planetary being," I smiled. "I'm sure they've got it under control."

At least, I hoped they did.

DOTTIE

"What are you going to call that sappy stuff you harvested?" Jalok asked. "Goop?"

"I think blood is the most straightforward thing to say until we have an in-depth analysis of what it's comprised of," I replied.

"You're funny when you speak rationally."

"How else am I supposed to speak?" I chuckled. "By the way, you've become a remarkably accomplished pilot in the last two hours."

"I don't know about accomplished but I've had extensive aerial training." Jalok looked over my shoulder with a smirk.

"Asshole!" I barked out a laugh and smacked him on the shoulder. "So that bumpy landing was just to rattle me?"

"I have to do something for entertainment. Scientists are incredibly boring."

"I take offense to that!"

"You were never in any danger," Jalok assured me. "Watch this."

He landed the aerial unit with feather-light grace.

"Was that supposed to make me less annoyed with you?"

"No. I just wanted to prove that I know what I'm doing."

Jalok hopped out of the unit and extended his hand to help me down.

"I'm going to take these samples back to the lab for analysis. Want to come?" I offered.

"I am obligated to do my duty and protect you," he replied.

"Oh that's right," I said with a face. You *have* to be around me."

"It's not that," he protested.

He would have said more but he saw the mischievous look in my eyes as I stuck my tongue at him.

"*Sk'lar to Jalok,*" his comm system abruptly interrupted us with a crackle.

Jalok looked at me as I waited for him. He walked off a bit as he began to discuss matters with his superior.

Eventually I gave up.

"I'll meet you in the lab," I said quietly, getting his attention. "I need to go!"

Unable to leave his conversation, Jalok reluctantly nodded.

"I'll be there soon," he whispered. "Stick to the main roads. No alleys."

"You got it." I gave him a thumbs-up.

"I'll swing by the lab when I'm done."

"See you later."

I left the camp at a brisk pace, eager to ship off the blood. I took some extra samples for my own analysis. There was always a chance it could lead to a breakthrough in my project.

"Where's your burly bodyguard?" Eluna asked when I swiped into the building.

"He has other jobs besides watching me," I replied.

"I stand by what I said this morning. I think you two like each other."

"That's nice. I have plant blood to test."

"Plant blood?"

I shrugged. "I also need these samples sent to the lab in Nyhiem. I've already written out the packing slip." I placed the samples and the packing slips on Eluna's desk.

"I'm still hung up on the plant blood thing."

"I know, it's weird. But since the Puppet Master

insists it's not exactly sap, we don't have a better name for it yet. Might as well keep things simple why we still can, right?"

"Is that why you won't admit that you like the Skotan?" Eluna gave me a conspiratorial look.

"In time, I might consider said Skotan a friend. I've made friends with an ancient being that brings life to our planet. Being friends with a Skotan doesn't seem daunting after that." I shrugged.

"But we're talking about a specific Skotan, one you wanted to kill the first time you brought him here," she pointed out.

"It's safe to say that I no longer want to kill him," I laughed.

"Because you like him."

And, I wasn't going there. No matter that those little flutters were getting stronger.

"Because he's tolerable," I corrected. "Please mail the samples for me? It'd be great if they arrived tomorrow."

"I'll see what I can do. Pillie at the postal service owes me a favor." Eluna winked.

"I don't want to know," I chuckled before heading back to the main lab.

My department was nine floors up.

Technically, Dr. Kroner ran our department even though I was Dr. Crane's right hand. If I wanted to run the department, I would've fought for it.

Lucky for Dr. Kroner, I wanted to remain in the field and work on my special projects. I was too young to run a department from a corner office.

"The planet whisperer returns," my co-worker Anita chirped when I walked in. "Where's that bodyguard?"

"Why is everyone so interested in Jalok?" I made my way to an open desk and pulled out my samples of the Puppet Master's blood.

"Because he's hot," Anita said bluntly. I almost knocked over one of my samples.

"You okay?" Another co-worker, Jett, asked.

"All good."

"What's that stuff anyway?"

"Plant blood. Yes, I know that's incorrect but that's just what I'm calling it until I figure out what's in it."

"You can use the mass spectrometer when I'm done," Jett offered.

"Thanks. Hopefully, that'll give me a starting point."

"You didn't answer my question," Anita pressed. "Where's the hot bodyguard?"

"Do you really think Jalok's hot?" I asked.

"We all do."

I turned to Jett in disbelief.

"Don't look at me. I like my partners human," he shrugged. "Not that I have anything against the aliens. I don't support those radicals. I just don't want to fuck any of the aliens."

"Thanks for the clarification," I chuckled.

"Well, I'd fuck him," Anita shrugged.

"That's not a surprise," my colleague, Raleigh, said snidely as she brushed past Anita's desk.

"Put the fangs away, Ra," Anita tutted.

"If you need to get laid, Ra, I humbly offer my services." Dyrn, a lab tech, strolled by.

"Try and I'll stick a pipette in a place a pipette should never be." She glanced down at his groin region to punctuate her threat.

"This is why I spent my days talking with the Puppet Master," I laughed. "You all need to get out more. Or less. Something!"

"No way an ancient, all-powerful, mystery of the ages is more entertaining than we are." Anita flashed a winning smile.

"More entertaining? No. More civilized? Absolutely."

I prepared my samples for several types of analysis while my lab mates bickered around me.

"So," Anita leaned over onto my desk. "Did you bang the bodyguard yet?"

"What is it with you and Eluna?" I groaned.

"Eluna's talked to you about him too?" Anita grinned.

"Yes. Twice now."

"Glad I'm not the only one who sees it. When you

two are in the room, you can cut the sexual tension with a knife."

"That's just wishful thinking on your part." I placed a tiny droplet of the Puppet Master's blood on a slide and placed it under the microscope.

"You're telling me you've never fooled around with him? Hasn't he been staying at your apartment?"

"Yes, he is and no we haven't." I adjusted the magnification. Nothing I saw looked familiar to me which was both equal parts frustrating and exciting. I removed the slide and carefully cleaned it, trying to focus on my work, and not the memory of his broad, shirtless chest.

"Should that be foaming?" Anita asked as the cleaning agent came into contact with the Puppet Master's blood.

"Definitely not." I quickly washed the slide with water and noted the blood's reaction with the cleaning agent.

Trying, and failing.

"I still can't believe you haven't made a move at the bodyguard."

"This really is a hot-button issue for you, isn't it?" I asked. "If I tell you that we kind-of-sort-of-not-really kissed will that get you off my back?"

"Absolutely not!" Anita squealed. "You have to tell me everything. How did it happen?"

"What happened?" Dyrn called from across the lab space.

"Dottie kissed the bodyguard."

"That's great!" Dyrn said. I gave him a quizzical look.

"Dottie, you have to admit it's been a while since you did anything that didn't involve your work. I have K'ver friend who's the same way. You'll never meet someone more dedicated. I was just telling him over a beer the other night that he needs to--"

Dyrn suddenly paused.

"He needs to what?" I prompted without looking up from my samples.

"He needs to die."

"What?" I looked up. Dyrn didn't look right. His skin was paler and covered in a sheen of sweat. His eyes were wild and unsettling, darting around the room like he was watching a fly.

"He needs to die. They all need to die. They're scum sucking the life out of our planet and they need to die!"

"What the fuck is wrong with you?" Anita stood up and backed away.

"Calm down, dude. Are you feeling okay?" Jett moved closer to Dyrn, arms outstretched.

"Are you one of them?" Dyrn twisted his neck in an unnatural way to look at Jett.

"Am I one of what? You really need to lie down."

"An alien lover!" Dyrn wailed. He whirled around and pointed at me with a shaking hand. "She's one of them. She admits that she kissed him."

"We need a medic in here now," I ordered. "I think he's been exposed to an airborne toxin or something."

"Get the gas masks on," Anita ordered.

Raleigh dashed out of the room to alert someone while Jett, Anita and I pulled on emergency masks. While I was adjusting my mask, Dyrn launched himself at me. He landed hard on the desks, clawing at me with his hands.

I leaped back, desperate to put as much between him and I as I could but he just kept scrambling. His clammy fingers latched around my arm.

I ripped myself away but as I did, he dug his nails in hard enough to tear the fabric of my lab coat.

"Dyrn!" I shouted. "Stop and think. You don't have to do this."

"I have to do my part to cleanse my planet," Dyrn growled.

"You're doing a terrible job." I turned at the sound of Jalok's voice.

"Are you alright?" he asked me, voice grim.

I nodded. "Just try not to kill Dyrn," I requested. "I don't know what's going on, but he's not really like this!"

Jalok nodded and moved quickly so he was between me and Dyrn.

Upon seeing Jalok, Dyrn spiraled deeper into a rage.

"I'll kill every last one of you if I have to." Dyrn leaped at Jalok, who dodged with ease.

"That's not a fight you're going to win," Jalok warned. "All you're doing is hurting your own people."

"Stop messing with my mind!" Dyrn screamed. He grabbed at the vials strewn about his workspace, uncapped one, and threw its contents at Jalok.

Jalok shouted in pain. I winced as his skin reacted to whatever Dyrn threw at him.

From the looks of it, it was some kind of acid. Dyrn threw vial after vial, burning Jalok more with each toss.

"I won't stop," Dyrn threatened. "I don't care what it takes. I won't stop until you're all dead at my feet."

With a snarl, Jalok rushed forward and grabbed Dyrn by the waist. He threw Dyrn across the room. Dyrn landed hard, but pulled himself to his feet, ready to attack again.

"Just stop," Jalok yelled. "You can't win this!"

Dyrn charged again, then stumbled over the rubble from the desk. Arms flailing, he lost his footing and fell back - right through a partially open window.

Jalok lunged forward, clutching at Dyrn's outstretched arms, but it was too late.

Dyrn screamed until we heard him hit the ground.

JALOK

"I'm fine," I said, but no one seemed to care.

I tried to hold on to a table, but my fingers felt limp and lifeless. They skidded over the slick surface, and I lost my balance. The ground rushed up to meet me at break-neck speed, and I hit it so hard the whole building seemed to shake underneath me.

Every single inch of my body felt like it was on fire, and I grimaced as I felt sharp stabs of pain.

Dottie knelt beside me but, even though my eyes were wide open, the most I could see was a vague silhouette.

"Oh, God," I heard her say, her voice sounding as if it was coming at me from the other side of the galaxy. I couldn't think straight, and it took all of my brain power to decode the meaning behind her words. "Jalok! Are you okay?"

"I'm...I'm fine..." I tried to say between hard breaths, and that even though I felt like miniature thermonuclear explosions were happening underneath my skin. I gritted my teeth so harshly I wouldn't have been surprised to hear them shatter under the pressure.

I balled my hands into fists then, the urge to scratch myself an overwhelming one. Every inch of my body itched, and it was taking all of my willpower not to peel my own skin off.

"The paramedics are on their way," Dottie cried out, but I couldn't really understand any of the words leaving her mouth.

The pain was so fierce that it felt like a thousand needles had been pushed against my brain, their sharp ends numbing everything but the suffering.

I deployed my scales on instinct, but that only seemed to make it all worse. Searing pain shot up from underneath them with a vengeance, and every single joint and ligament on my body felt like it was burning from the inside out.

I closed my eyes and clenched my jaw, oblivious to whatever was going on around me.

The acid ate into my skin hungrily, and I knew it would only be a matter of time until my body gave out.

I remembered Dottie saying something about paramedics, but I didn't hang my hopes on it.

Even if they got here on time, it'd be a matter of luck. Dyrn had thrown so much shit my way that my skin had to be like the counter of a bar on a busy Saturday night.

Skrell, I thought, *not like this.*

It took all I had not to pass out.

Pushing myself off the floor, I sat against a wall and opened my eyes.

Dottie remained kneeling by my side, her eyes brimming with tears.

I didn't want her to see this, but I didn't want her to leave.

Of course. Nothing had made sense, not since I found her in that alleyway.

"Move aside, move aside," I heard a chorus of voices repeat, and then there were gloved hands on my body. I groaned as someone forced me to lay down, and a pair of quick moving hands rolled me onto a stretcher.

I kept my eyes open as I was carted out of the lab, but I couldn't even register where I was going. The hallways looked all the same, and the human faces peering down at me all shared the same concerned look.

Suddenly, the bland ceiling of the hallways was

replaced by a bright blue sky, and I closed my eyes as that brightness burnt my brain.

"Steady now," someone said, and the stretcher was lifted up and onto something. I didn't need to open my eyes to know that I was in the back of an emergency hovercraft.

The pungent smell of antiseptic hit me like a brick, and that only helped the swaying motion of the hovercraft in making me nauseous.

I tried to sit up, but a dozen hands pushed me back onto the stretcher, all while someone placed a breathing mask over my mouth.

"Don't move now," another voice said, and then someone held my arm as I tried to rip the breathing mask off my face. "You're gonna feel a little sting."

I didn't feel anything.

I noticed the needle going under one of my scales and pushing through my skin, but there was no actual pain.

It was as if I was under a metric ton of anesthetics...except these anesthetics made it feel like my body was burning from the inside out.

"Dottie...Dottie..." It was my own voice, but I didn't even recognize it.

It came out throaty and garbled, sounding foreign to my own ears, and every word that spilled out from between my lips felt like lava.

I didn't even know if Dottie was in there with me but, somehow, that was the only thing I cared about.

I endured the ride as well as I could, slipping in and out of consciousness. All around me nurses and doctors screamed out their orders as they wheeled me through hospital corridors, and I suddenly realized that I was already out of the emergency transport.

"You're going to be just fine," a man wearing blue scrubs told me, but I didn't trust his words. I didn't feel like I was going to be fine. My skin seemed to be melting off, and I was in so much pain that to think rationally was an impossible mission. "We've put you on some pretty strong painkillers, so you'll start feeling better in a couple of minutes. You might feel a bit drowsy, but it's going to be fine. Just hang in there, alright?"

"*Kavnash aher,*" I groaned, the old Skotan military salute somehow jumping to the front of my mind. I was trying to speak to the medical staff, but my brain had already dove off the deep end.

Clenching my jaw, I forced my eyelids up and tried to regain my bearings. I could hear the constant beeping of some machine beside me, nurses reading off their charts, hurried footsteps...and then there was nothing.

Absolutely nothing.

My body felt so light I was almost afraid I would

float up, and the hospital bed I was laying in was adrift in never-ending darkness. Sitting up, I stared into the void. In the distance, I could see two figures drifting toward me.

They were as tall as I was, the two of them donning military uniforms, and I felt my heart tightening as I recognized my father and grandfather.

"Father," I muttered, but he just glared at me, his expression one of contempt.

"*You're no son of mine.*" He didn't move his lips, but his voice reached me all the same. "*You're an embarrassment. Look at the state you're in.*"

"*It didn't even happen on the battlefield,*" my grandfather said. Instead of contempt, there was disappointment in his voice. That hurt even more. "*You were meant for great things. You were meant to be a warrior. But look at you now.*"

"I am a warrior," I tried to say, but as I opened my mouth no words came out. My tongue felt as heavy as lead, and my lips were suddenly sewn together.

The two of them just looked at me, their contempt and disappointment like two lethal bullets, and then I heard a metallic sound cut through the silence.

It was rhythmic and heavy, echoing inside my head like thunder, and I turned my face to see an old human walking toward me, a cane in his hands.

He slammed the tip of the cane against an invisible

floor with each step he took, and he stopped right at the foot of my bed. I had no idea who he was, but his face reminded me of Dottie.

Even though I couldn't tell how I knew it, that was her grandfather. Great, great, something.

"You stay away from Dottie, you hear me?" The old man said, and I watched in horror as his eyes turned black. *"You're not a warrior, nor are you a good man. You're just a worthless thug. Stay away from Dottie. She's too good for you."*

"No...no..." I breathed out, over and over again, and the bed I was in started sinking into the darkness.

Suddenly, there was water all around me, and it rushed up my body until I was struggling to keep my head above it.

Struggling, I did my best to breathe, but that just made me swallow more and more of that dark water.

I was drowning.

Not like this, I thought before I passed out, *not like this.*

Then, right before I drifted off, I cried out.

"Dottie!"

DOTTIE

The lab was closed today for obvious reasons. A grief counselor was on standby for any of the staff, particularly in my department.

But a sit down with a grief counselor wasn't the reason I was awake at the crack of dawn that morning. I'd barely slept. I tossed and turned all night.

Jalok was seriously injured. He'd been taken from my lab building by his own team and I wasn't allowed to follow him to make sure he was okay.

Technically, he was my bodyguard not the other way around, but I couldn't stand the thought of not knowing what was happening.

Jalok got hurt because he was protecting me.

This was all my fault.

By the time the sun came up over the skyline, Not wanting to deal with any hassles, I went out my fire escape and walked into the base camp, leaving the Skotan soldier who was my replacement bodyguard standing outside my front door.

"Dr. Bellin." A K'ver greeted me with a nod and a confused look.

"Sk'lar right?"

"Yes, ma'am. I lead Strike Team Three. Jalok's team," he explained.

"How is he?" I asked.

"I can't tell you. He was transported to the hospital inside out offices in Nyhiem."

My stomach dropped and twisted. If he had to be taken back to the capital, he must've really been hurt.

"He was in that bad of shape?"

"I'm afraid so. I haven't heard anything since the medical team took him. But that's a good thing," Sk'lar added quickly. "It means he's still alive."

I allowed myself to take a breath.

"Do you know if the doctors are letting him see visitors?" I asked.

"I don't. But the Doctor, Dr. Evie Parr, is one of the most compassionate people I've ever met. At the very least, she'll allow you to talk to her directly about his progress."

"What if I brought her information?" An idea struck me like a bolt.

"Such as?"

"The chemicals Dyrn threw on Jalok were created in the lab. Dyrn probably kept notes when he created them. I could bring the notes to Dr. Parr in exchange for a visitation."

"I wouldn't phrase it like that but I think Dr. Parr will welcome any information you can give." Sk'lar tried to laugh but it didn't sound right.

"I promise not to hold information hostage."

Sk'lar and I shook hands.

"Where is your bodyguard?" he asked me all of a sudden. "I had assigned Dorek to cover for Jalok."

"Right," I blurted, not wanting to admit I'd dodged him at home. "I think I just saw him. I'll go get him."

Before Sk'lar could say anything I headed, out of the base. My lab was technically closed but the building wasn't locked up.

I swiped in and took the stairs to my floor. Only an underpaid security guard milled about. He didn't even ask me for ID.

I triple checked to make sure everything was locked up before going over to Dyrn's desk. Everything was exactly how he left it.

No doubt an investigation had been launched.

Careful not to disturb anything, I logged in to his console.

Finding his notes was easy. Everything on his console was clearly labeled. It led me to believe that Dyrn didn't plan his attack.

In one sense, that was a relief. I wasn't working side by side with a violent radical all these years.

Unfortunately, this realization left me with more questions. If he wasn't planning on hurting anyone, what would possess him to change so drastically in a matter of seconds?

I set the notes to my datapad and fled the lab. I didn't want to be here anymore. As I walked past the front desk, the phone rang.

No one should be calling a closed lab. Out of curiosity, I answered it.

"Dr. Bellin."

"Good, I caught you." I recognized Sk'lar's voice.

"Do you need something from the lab?" I asked.

"No. I wanted to tell you to return to the command center." A knot tightened in my stomach.

Sk'lar got the call that Jalok died.

That's why he needed me to come back.

Jalok, brave, funny, infuriating Jalok.

"I've arranged transport for you to Nyhiem with one of my best fliers."

Oh.

I let out a shaky breath.

"Are you all right, Dr. Bellin?"

"Yes. Sorry. Thank you. I'll be there shortly." I hung up the phone and braced myself against the desk. My legs shook under my weight.

Why was I so shaken?

I forced the uneasiness away and walked out of the lab.

A two-person aerial unit and a Valorni pilot were waiting for me.

"You Dr. Bellin?"

"Yes."

"Great. Hop in. Have you flown in one of these before?"

"Yes." I climbed into the back seat without assistance.

The Valorni climbed in after me and powered up the aerial unit. We didn't make small talk as we flew.

No joking, laughing or taunting like I did with Jalok. I leaned back in my seat and pulled out my datapad.

I killed time on the flight by going over the notes on the chemicals Dyrn developed. They were unusual and I couldn't discern why he was making such mixtures.

Maybe he was planning something after all. That still didn't explain his sudden and drastic personality shift.

Anger welled up inside me.

Anger wouldn't serve me so, to quell it, I flipped to my own projects on the datapad. The Puppet Master's data was just as obscure to me now as it was yesterday.

I didn't even get to test his blood.

I wished I could talk to the Puppet Master now.

After a few hours, the Valorni pilot safely landed on the roof of General Rouhr's operations building.

"Thanks!" I called over my shoulder as I ran to the door leading down to the lower floors. Finding the hospital wasn't difficult. Hospitals look the same no matter what species they serve.

"I'm looking for Dr. Evie Parr," I announced when I entered the medical suite.

"I'm Dr. Parr. How did you get back here?" A petite woman with blonde hair frowned.

"I have information about the chemicals used to burn Jalok." I handed her the datapad.

"You're the scientist he was assigned to guard," she said with a knowing smile.

"Yes, he was injured protecting me." My stomach clenched. My fault. "Can I see him?"

"Yes and no." Dr. Parr looked at me with sorrow in her blue eyes.

"What do you mean?"

"We've stabilized him but we had to put him in a coma to do so."

"What?" I yelped. My legs started to tremble again.

Dr. Parr's face blurred as little pricks of light clouded my vision.

"You need to sit down." Dr. Parr grabbed my arm and lead me to what I assumed was a chair. I wasn't paying attention to what my body did.

"A coma?" I sputtered.

"Drink this."

A straw prodded at my lips. I took a sip and struggled to swallow.

"The chemicals mixed into a toxin that seeped right into his bloodstream. They made their way into his brain. We had to subdue him," Dr. Parr explained.

"Is he going to be okay?"

"He's responding positively to the treatment." Dr. Parr's words were meant to be encouraging but I knew it was just an optimistic version of 'I don't know'.

"Can I see him?"

"Of course. I'll walk you in." Dr. Parr linked her arm through mine and walked me through the medical suite.

We stopped at the last bed in the row. Dr. Parr pulled back the privacy curtain. At the sight of Jalok, I covered my mouth and looked away.

Most of his upper body was covered in bandages. Only his right arm was left exposed. It was covered in oozing, blistering wounds.

"Those are too severe to wrap at the moment," Dr.

Parr explained when she noticed me staring. "He's going to have scars for life on that arm."

"He might like that," I laughed awkwardly.

Dr. Parr chuckled.

"You're right. These soldiers love their battle scars."

Jalok was hooked up to a machine that looked like it was simultaneously pumping blood into him and harvesting it from him.

"What's that?"

"It's a blood detox, essentially. We're removing his blood, flushing it of toxins and putting it back. It's our best bet at the moment. Operating directly on his brain is far too dangerous right now."

"But that's a possibility?"

"One we're hoping we won't have to face. Strong, healthy blood should target lingering toxins."

"Right." I gave a jerky nod.

"Go ahead and sit with him for a while. He might like it if you talk to him."

"Can he hear me?"

"I like to think so." Dr. Parr waited for me to settle myself into the chair beside Jalok's bed before closing the privacy curtain.

"I don't think sorry covers it," I laughed weakly. "I'm sorry for laughing, too. I can't help it. If I don't laugh, I'm going to start crying. I don't like to cry in front of strangers. They start asking questions and trying to help. But they can't help. Not unless they can fix you and wake you up."

Tears pricked the backs of my eyes. I blinked them back with little success.

"Why did you have to be a hero?" I asked him.

My gaze wandered over Jalok's various injuries and all of the machines he was hooked up to.

I wanted to grab his hand to let him know I was there in case he couldn't hear me but his hand looked too damaged.

I didn't want to hurt him further.

"You need to wake up soon. I need to yell at you for causing me so much emotional distress."

I was already imagining all of the retorts Jalok would launch at me if that conversation ever took place. I really hoped it would take place soon.

Exhaustion settled over me. Aside from the brief periods of restless sleep I got last night, I'd been wide awake since Dyrn attacked.

I scooted my chair closer and rested my head on the edge of Jalok's bed.

Of course, I was upset that something so horrible happened to my friend.

But when I looked at Jalok, lying there and hooked up to all those machines, my feelings weren't the feelings that someone had for their friend.

I felt a deep sense of loss that made me feel hopeless.

Every time I looked at his scarred, bandaged face I thought about our kiss.

The notion that I might never get to do that again filled me with sorrow I didn't understand it at all.

I was still thinking about his lips and his laugh when I drifted off to sleep on the edge of his hospital bed.

JALOK

"Dottie!" Sitting up straight on the bed, I reached for a gun that wasn't there and quickly scanned the room, expecting to see a dozen Xathi crawling toward me. There were no Xathi in the room, of course.

There was also no sign of Dottie.

"Whoa, calm down," Rokul said, laying a hand on my shoulder. I grimaced as pain radiated from the place where his fingers met my skin, and he withdrew his hand quickly. He threw me a concerned glance and lowered his voice. "Sorry. I forgot."

"That's fine," I groaned, sucking in a deep breath.

I was in a cramped hospital room, and Rokul and Sk'lar were sitting beside me in tiny plastic chairs.

I could see Sk'lar's chair perfectly, but I only

assumed Rokul was sitting in one. He was so massive that I couldn't even see what was underneath him.

He had been one of the biggest guys aboard the *Vengeance*, and he looked like a giant whenever he stood beside a human. "Where's Dottie? Is she alright?"

"Dottie's fine, yes," Sk'lar said. "You don't need to worry about her. You saved her, remember?"

"I did, didn't I?" I muttered. Pinching the bridge of my nose, I tried to reach for the cloudy memories hiding in my mind's fog.

I remembered Dyrn's mental breakdown, his voice growing angrier all out of a sudden, but I didn't remember much beyond it. Nothing but pain. "What happened to the—"

"Dyrn? The crazy scientist?" Rokul jumped in. "He's dead."

"Dead?"

"Yes," he nodded. "At least he was the last time I checked."

"Did I kill him?"

"Don't think," he shrugged. "The body is being autopsied as we speak, but I won't be terribly surprised if the cause of death turns out to be Angry Skotan Syndrome. But never mind that right now. How are you feeling?"

"Like shit," I groaned, carefully laying back on the

mattress. My body was sore, and I was feeling so itchy it was a struggle not to rip the bandages off my body.

Each movement I made sent pain up my spine, and I had such a bad headache that my eyes felt like they would pop out of their sockets any time now. "What do the doctors say?"

"We're here for the funeral, actually," Sk'lar said, but he shut up really quickly after Rokul elbowed him.

That made me smile and, even though something as stupid as a simple smile hurt like a gut wound, it still made me feel better about the whole thing. "They say you'll be fine. Your arm is going to be scarred, though. They couldn't do much about it."

"Whatever," I grunted.

Scars weren't a bad thing. They were the mark of a warrior. Humans didn't really appreciate it but, the way I saw it, the more the better. "How long have I been out for?"

"A couple of days," Sk'lar continued. "They had to put you into a coma. You were pretty screwed up. The chemicals blended together and slipped into your bloodstream. You were lucky Cazak was there."

"Cazak?"

"Yeah. You had to have a blood transfusion so that your blood could clear up."

"I don't remember any of that," I muttered, my eyes

closed as I tried to ignore the stubborn throbbing on the back of my head.

"Figures," Rokul said in that deep tone of his. "You were pretty out of it. Hallucinations, the doctors said. You were saying some pretty wild stuff."

"Like what?"

"You kept on begging for a weapon," he shrugged. "And vowed to kill every single Xathi in the universe. You know, your regular Monday morning mood."

"You're hilarious, Rokul."

Pinching the bridge of my nose, I felt all those hallucinations and nightmares bubbling up to the surface.

There was a stab of pain in my heart as I remembered both my father and grandfather, the disappointment they had shown during my hallucinations suddenly feeling very real.

Even Dottie's family had shown up in my nightmares, all of them accusing me of being a failure at my job.

The only thing in my dreams that hadn't brought me any pain had been Dottie.

Memories of her smile helped me cling to whatever sanity still resided inside me. Even though I couldn't exactly prove it, I knew she was the reason I was now conscious.

I sighed, feeling like a hollow version of my old self.

I forced my eyes open and ran one hand through my hair. Groaning, I reached for the glass of water resting on the bed stand and took a small sip.

The water felt like the most amazing thing I had ever tasted as it went down my dry throat, and I suddenly realized I was ravenous.

"I need to eat something," I said, but Sk'lar and Rokul immediately exchanged a knowing glance.

"Sorry, man, you'll have to take it easy for a day or two," Rokul said. "They've been feeding you through an IV drip, and it'll take some time before your stomach adjusts to some real food."

"Just perfect."

"Cheer up," Sk'lar chuckled. "You'll be up and running in no time. I mean, the doctors told us it could take up to two weeks before you regained your consciousness...and here you are now, already bitching about your situation after only a couple of days."

"I'm not—"

"Of course not," he laughed. Slowly, he stood up from his chair and gave me a nod. "I'll come around later today, alright? I have a meeting in about fifteen minutes. You comin', Rokul?"

"I'm right behind you," Rokul replied. "I just want to discuss something with Jalok first."

"Got it." Clicking his heels together, Sk'lar stepped out of the bedroom and closed the door behind him.

The constant chatter of a busy hospital corridor slipped into the room during the brief moment the door remained open, but it vanished the moment the latch fell into place again.

"What's the matter?" I asked, worried that they hadn't been telling me the whole truth about what had happened. "Is this about Dottie? Is she alright?"

"She's fine," he nodded, but the barely noticeable smile on his face was enough to make me relax. "We found her brother, Adam Bellin."

"You did? Where is he?" I sat up on the bed so fast that my brain waltzed inside my skull.

Grimacing, I tried to keep my waning focus on Rokul. I hadn't really expected for Adam to be found alive, and so these were great news.

"He's in a refugee camp outside Duvest."

"That's good, isn't it?"

"I think so," he nodded. "But there's something you have to know about him."

"Oh, please don't tell me he's one of those anti-alien assholes?" My headache seemed to become a dozen times worse. If Dottie's brother turned out to be some xenophobic creep, that would be an annoying turn of events.

"Not exactly. He hasn't joined any anti-alien movement...but he isn't exactly a fan of what we do."

"That's not so bad," I whispered.

I didn't care much about those unwilling to pick sides, but I could make an exception for Dottie's brother.

Truth be told, his political affiliations didn't even really matter. What mattered was that I had found her lost brother, and that was sure to make her happy.

And that...well, *that* mattered. "Have you reached out to him?"

"Not yet," Rokul replied. "But we have eyes on him. Just say the word and we'll make a reunion happen."

"Good," I nodded. "Do it."

DOTTIE

I sat at my desk back in Kaster staring blandly at the scrolls of data on my console screen, seeing nothing. All I could think about was Jalok.

Unfortunately, I had to work today. I planned on leaving early to return to Nyhiem by nightfall but the experiments I was running were taking longer to process than I'd anticipated.

I paced the length of my lab in a restless flurry.

"You almost knocked over my datapads," Anita said as I stormed by for the nine-hundredth time that hour.

"Sorry." I forced myself to stop moving and pressed my fingers against my eyelids. "I can't sit still."

"No kidding," Anita snorted. "What's the matter? Are you trying to get up to Nyhiem today?"

"Yeah. Jalok only woke up yesterday. I haven't heard

from Dr. Parr. I'm worried something's already gone wrong."

"What happened to 'no news is good news'?"

"That only applied when I didn't know if he was dead or not. Now, when I don't hear anything, I assume the worst has happened and no one wants to tell me because I'll be upset."

"You really like him, don't you?" Anita smiled. I decided to give her an honest answer.

"I don't know how I feel. I feel conflicted over everything."

"That's understandable." Anita reached out to rub my arm. "You've experienced a slew of super intense emotions this last week. It's only natural that you feel off balance."

"I don't like being off balance. And I don't like being here while Jalok could be relapsing," I groaned.

"If something was wrong, someone would reach out to you," Anita said firmly. "I'm sure of it."

"Be sure of it enough for both of us because I'm not sure about anything."

"Are you Dottie Bellin?" A deep voice came from the entrance to the lab.

"Oh my," Anita gasped.

Standing in the entryway was the largest being, human or alien, I'd ever seen.

He dwarfed Jalok which should've been impossible.

"I'm Dottie. Yes." I stuttered, still trying to comprehend why a giant red alien was asking after me. My confusion turned to horror. "What's wrong? Is Jalok all right?"

"He's fine. Still on bedrest."

"Right." I breathed a sigh of relief. "What can I do for you?"

"Come with me, please." The Skotan giant turned his back and strode away.

"What's that all about?" Anita asked.

"I have no idea. Watch my stuff?"

"Sure thing." Anita wasn't looking at me. She was following the Skotan giant with a hungry look in her eyes.

I chuckled as I jogged after the Skotan. "Not to be rude," I spoke when I caught up to him. "But who are you?"

"My name is Rokul." He said nothing more.

"Great. Where are we going?"

"I'm taking you to the Silver Whale."

"Why?"

The Silver Whale was the oldest restaurant in Kaster. It used to be nothing more than a wooden shack where fishermen would go to warm up after a day at sea. Now, it was rather grand.

"You'll see."

"Are you trying to be unsettling on purpose? Because you're doing a marvelous job."

"Thank you." I caught his smirk.

We walked through the doors of the Silver Whale. It'd been years since I'd set foot inside. The polish hardwood floors gleamed. Parts of old ships still decorated the walls.

"I still don't understand why-"

Then I saw him.

Sitting at the smallest table in the back corner of the restaurant, looking out the window.

"Adam." I breathed.

I looked at Rokul.

"You knew he was here?"

"Go greet your brother. I'll be nearby."

Excitement welled up inside me. I thought I was going to burst from it.

"Adam" I shouted.

My brother looked away from the window. A blinding smile spread across his face as he leaped up from his seat. I ran through the dining floor not caring if I knocked into tables or patron's shoulders.

Adam opened his arms. I jumped up just like I used to when I was a kid. He hugged me so tightly that my ribs ached but I didn't care.

"I can't believe it," I gasped. There was something

wet on my face. I pulled away to tap my cheeks. I was crying. "I thought you were dead."

"Let's have a seat and I'll tell you everything." Adam pressed a kiss into the top of my head and lead me to his table in the corner. I was so excited I could barely make myself sit down.

"Want something to eat?" Adam offered.

"I couldn't possibly eat at a time like this." I bounced in my seat. "I could go for a cup of coffee, though."

"You're literally vibrating with excitement. Coffee is definitely not happening."

"Good point. Where have you been? Why haven't I heard from you sooner?"

"When the Xathi attacked Fraga, I gathered as many people as I could and snuck them out of the city. We spent weeks in the jungle dodging Xathi patrols and rabid creatures. I would've contacted you if I could, but I had reason to suspect the Xathi could monitor radio frequencies. Besides, for a long time, I didn't know if you were dead or alive either."

"When the Xathi came to Kaster, I hid," I said quietly. "I regret hiding. I should've done more to help people. I should've been more like you."

"Because you hid, you survived. Because you survived, you're here to do important research that might help our planet bounce back."

"You know about my work?" I smiled.

"The big guy filled me in a little bit on the way here."

"What did you do after the Xathi invasion ended?"

"Well, we were in the jungle pretty far from any city or settlement. It took us a while to understand that the Xathi weren't a threat anymore. After a few weeks of quietness, we ventured to the city closest to us. Duvest. We were filled in on everything that had happened. The first thing I did was check the lists of the dead and missing for your name. When I saw that you were alive and accounted for, I'd never felt more relief in my life."

"Why didn't you contact me?"

The initial excitement of seeing my brother ebbed to make room for a sense of hurt. Adam's been alive for months and it took him this long to reach out.

"Duvest was a disaster. An alien warship crashed into the city. I had no way to contact you. I didn't know how to reach you," Adam explained.

"You could've come home," I frowned.

"I wanted to." Adam's eyes were pleading. "But there were people who still needed my help. I was finally able to do what I was born to do, what I joined the Search and Rescue crew for. They needed care, they needed homes. It was my duty to help give that to them. I knew you were safe. If for one moment I thought that you weren't, I would've come immediately. You believe me don't you?"

"A riot broke out here in Kaster," I said. "I was in danger then."

"The riot wasn't reported right away. When I heard about it, I packed my bags and started heading to Kaster. That's when the big guy found me." Adam nodded in Rokul's direction.

"He was looking for you?" I furrowed my brow. "Why?"

"I actually don't know. But when an alien that big walks up to you and says follow me, you listen."

"Apparently, he does that for dramatic effect," I rolled my eyes. "He did the same thing to me."

"Interesting. But don't you see, Dottie. I was coming for you. I just can't get around as easily as some. I don't have my own means of transport. I've been relying on shuttles and lifts from kind strangers. You believe me, right?"

I looked at Adam's face.

He looked so desperate for me to believe him.

"As far as excuses go," I sighed, "not contacting me because you were helping people rebuild their lives after an alien invasion is a pretty good one."

"I knew you'd understand."

For a moment, I just rested in the warmth of his presence. My brother was home. Jalok was recovering.

All was right with the world.

Unless…

"Speaking of aliens," I lowered my voice. "I need to know how you feel about them."

"Do we really need to go there?"

His answer made me uneasy.

"I'm under near-constant guard because of the anti-alien radicals. Yes, we have to go there."

"Look, I won't lie to you. I'm not the biggest fan of the aliens," he admitted. "They brought the Xathi to us. I know it was an accident, but still, it happened. Now, they're inadvertently sparking riots. I realize that's not their fault either but let's face it. Even if they have the best intentions, they bring destruction. I don't support the people calling for their deaths but I think our planet would be better off if they left."

"That's fair, I suppose," I nodded. "I'm friends with some of them. Is that a problem?"

"As long as they don't get you hurt or killed, they're fine in my book."

"Good," I grinned. "Why did Rokul go looking for you?"

"When I finally worked up the guts to ask him, he said you wanted to see me," Adam shrugged. "Isn't that true?"

I leaned back, shocked, mind circling frantically for an answer.

"Of course, I wanted to see you but I've never met Rokul in my life. I don't know how he'd know about you." The realization hit me before I finished the sentence. "Hey, Rokul?"

The burly Skotan stood up and walked over to our table.

"How did you know about Adam?" I asked.

Rokul smirked.

"Jalok gave me a name and pointed me in the right direction. He would've gone himself but he took a chemical shower."

"Jalok found Adam?"

Rokul nodded and sauntered back to where he sat before.

"Jalok's a friend of yours?" Adam asked.

When I looked back at Adam, tears were slipping down my cheeks again.

"Something like that."

JALOK

For days I found it a struggle to simply drag myself from the hospital bed to the nearby lavatory.

A week ago I was flinging large humans about as if they were infants. But after the chemical attack, I had been reduced to a pathetic, near helpless state.

At one point, early in my recovery, I'd stubbornly refused to call for assistance, even though I could barely walk.

My legs gave out, and I wound up sprawled across the floor.

Again, I was too stubborn to ask for assistance and wound up laying there for hours until someone came to check on me.

Back when I was a youngling, it seemed like I could never get enough sleep.

Between training at the Skotan military academy and my familial obligations, there just hadn't been enough time.

When I was recovering in the hospital after the chemical burns, all I did was sleep.

The novelty wore off rather quickly.

The most frustrating thing was lying there and watching the world go on without me.

Cazak and Navat came calling a couple of times, but listening to them speak about their duties only reinforced how miserable I was laid up on my back.

I was on the precipice of slumber, hanging on by a mere thread, when my door popped open.

Groggily, I rose up into a sitting position, expecting another nurse come to take my vitals.

To my surprise, Dottie came strolling in, accompanied by a human roughly her own age.

I took in his reddish hair, the cast of his eyes, and surmised that this young man must be her long lost brother, Adam.

"Hey, thug." Dottie came over to my bedside and squeezed my hand.

"Dottie." I smiled at her, though it was a struggle to remain conscious.

I looked past her at the man I took to be Adam. "And you have been reunited with your brother, I see."

"Yes, thanks to you." She squeezed my hand tighter

for a moment, then released it. Dottie gestured toward Adam. "Jalok, meet Adam. Adam, meet Jalok."

"A Skotan. I see." Adam's face had a smile etched on its surface, but the light didn't reach his cold gaze. "My sister tells me that you were instrumental in bringing us back together. Thank you."

"Yes, thank you so much, Jalok." Dottie squeezed Adam around the torso and sighed. "I thought I'd lost him forever."

"You have my gratitude for bringing me back to my sister, Jalok."

I felt a bit embarrassed by all of the gratitude.

"Oh, it was nothing." I waved my hand dismissively, hoping they wouldn't notice what even that simple movement cost me in terms of fatigue. "All I did was ask other people to do me a favor, that's all. I've been laid up here the whole time."

"Don't discount what you've done for me." Dottie put her hands on her hips, but the scowl on her face was purely for comical effect. "You just take your due credit like a man, mister."

"He's not a man, he's a Skotan."

We looked at Adam, an awkward silence stretching out into the room.

Abruptly Dottie cleared her throat and glared at her brother. "What's that supposed to mean? Got a problem with that?"

"No, of course not." Adam shook his head, and for a moment his gaze softened a bit when he stared at his sister. "I'm just pointing it out, that's all."

"Your human designation 'man' refers to a male of your species, correct?"

Adam and Dottie's gazes snapped over to me.

He seemed a bit amused, but Dottie had a worried frown wrinkling her otherwise cute face.

"Yes." Adam dragged out the last syllable of the word, as if suspicious of my intentions.

"Well, then, as I am a male of my species, I suppose you could call me a 'Skotan Man.' If you wished."

Adam grinned at that, but again he had a sinister cast to his eyes that said he wasn't mirthful or happy.

There was an edge to the man's demeanor that I didn't like, and not just because he seemed to have a problem with aliens.

The suspicious part of me wondered if he'd been involved with the riots, as ridiculous as that notion was. He'd been lost, far away from Kaster, hadn't he?

"So, Adam, Dottie tells me that you're a first responder."

"Why, yes, I am." Adam smiled at his sister, then at me. "I didn't used to get much action, but of course these days I keep quite busy."

"Yes, the Xathi attack was excellent job security for both of us."

We laughed at my weak joke, but the whole time our gazes were locked in a stare of suspicion.

It's as if both of us were waiting for the other shoe to drop, to turn a Terran phrase. I was reminded of a time after my family had relocated, and I'd introduced my new friends to my old friends. There had been tension there, too.

I wished at the time I could just chalk up my ill feelings to such a notion of unfamiliarity, but there was just something about Adam I couldn't bring myself to trust.

Nothing overt, nothing I could call him out on without seeming like a big jerk to Dottie, but definitely something.

And I didn't like him near her.

For a time the silence stretched on to an agonizing level, but then Adam's comm saved the day. He glanced at the screen and then looked apologetically toward his sister.

"I'm afraid I have to take this. Sorry."

"No, you're fine. I'll stay here and keep Jalok company."

Something about what she said didn't sit well with Adam. He shot me a suspicious glare and then headed out into the hallway to take his call.

Dottie turned back to me and smiled. She took my hand and pressed it between both of hers. Her grip felt warm, soft, and reassuring on my meaty paw.

"Are you in much pain?"

"Not so much anymore. Just some itching on my arm. Mostly, I'm just really tired."

"Should I leave and let you sleep?"

"No." I silently cursed at the near panic in my tone. "Stay a little longer, please. It's so dull here."

"I'll certainly stay for a bit, then, and entertain you."

Dottie began telling me about her research.

Truth to tell, most of it went over my head. I'm not a stupid man, no matter what Cazak might have told you, but I'm definitely a man of action.

Still, I liked hearing the sound of her voice no matter what she said.

Strange how a few days prior I'd found being around Dottie to be so confusing I'd have done almost anything to get away from her.

"So the Puppet Master thinks that the Ancient Enemies he knows of may not be the same as the ones in the Urai legends, because of the massive amount of time that has passed since then."

Dottie paused, and looked at me intently until I realized she was waiting for a response. Since I hadn't been paying much attention, lost in the corridors of my suspicion over Adam, I stammered through an answer.

"Ah, well, I suppose he is pretty old."

"That's true, but there are many mythologies from seemingly disparate cultures that have profound connections. Maybe by researching the Urai legends we can learn something about these 'ancient enemies.'"

"Maybe. I'll tell you what, Doctor Dottie, you figure out where and who the ancient enemies are, and I'll be more than happy to knock them on their butts."

She laughed, her eyes lighting up in a way that said she genuinely enjoyed my company. I wasn't sure what to make of that.

"It's a deal." The smile faded from her face, and she cleared her throat. "My assistant, the man who attacked you with acid, he uh—he didn't survive the fall."

I snorted, feeling a burst of anger for the man who had nearly maimed me.

"Good."

Dottie's face grew dark with anger, but she suppressed it quickly.

"I suppose you have good reason to feel that way, but it leaves us with a lot of unanswered questions."

"Like what kind of sound he'd have made if I'd torn his limbs off instead of thrown him out the window?"

"No." Dottie hid her face in her palm and sighed. "No, I mean, why did he suddenly change so radically like that? One second he was talking about his K'ver buddy, and the next he's an anti-alienist xenophobe so furious he has to attack a being twice his size? It doesn't make any sense."

I wanted to say that a lot of human behavior didn't make much sense, but I held my tongue.

At that point, the door opened once more and Adam strolled back into the room.

His eyes narrowed for a split second when he saw her holding my hand, but his smile replaced the sneer so quickly I don't think Dottie even noticed his initial reaction.

"All finished." He slipped his comm unit into an overall pocket and lifted his eyebrows when he turned to Dottie. "Are you ready, sister?"

"Yes, we should let Jalok rest."

I wanted to argue, but at that point I could barely keep my eyelids open.

As I leaned gratefully back into my bed, Dottie suddenly leaned forward and kissed me on the cheek.

"Thank you for giving me back my brother, Jalok."

I couldn't stop the goofy grin from crossing my face as she left the room, stopping for a final wave at the door.

Sighing, I settled into my comfortable prison and descended back into slumber.

When I dreamt, it was of Dottie and her warm, soft kisses.

DOTTIE

I left Jalok's bedside feeling better than I had in weeks. Everything felt like it was coming together.

Jalok's recovery was going smoothly. My brother was alive and back in my life.

The only thing missing was a breakthrough in my research on the Puppet Master.

"Are you Dottie Bellin?" A woman with short dark hair and more than her fair share of scars approached me as I left the medical suite.

"Yes," I answered slowly.

"My name's Tella." She stuck out her hand and gave mine a firm shake. My shoulder popped. "Sorry. Rokul tells me I'm too used to interacting with aliens."

"You're friends with Rokul?"

"We're together, actually." Tella's face softened into a happy smile.

Adam frowned slightly at that. Strange.

"The grip makes a lot more sense now," I laughed uneasily.

Tella released my hand. It hurt to curl my fingers in. "I should take up arm-wrestling with Jalok. It might toughen me up a bit."

"Are you and him a thing?" Tella asked with genuine interest.

"No, uh," I hesitated. I didn't know what Jalok and I were.

"I understand," Tella said with a knowing smile. "It's hard enough to explain when you're starting something with another human. It's a whole new beast when you're entering into something with an alien."

"We haven't entered into anything." My voice sounded robotic, and I carefully didn't look over at Adam.

"Right." Tella winked. "I didn't come up to you to hassle you about your interpersonal, intergalactic relationships. I'm a botanist. General Rouhr's botanist, actually."

"Oh," I brightened. A botanist. That sure explained all those scars. "Of course. I've read some of your notes on the Puppet Master."

"I'm sorry they weren't more helpful. I didn't actually know what I was dealing with."

"It was a good jumping off point before I began interacting with the Puppet Master directly. Once I started talking to him regularly previous notes weren't necessary."

"You talk to him?" Tella looked amazed.

"A few times a week if I can manage," I smiled. "It's been hectic lately but we keep in touch."

"You're talking about him like he's a friend."

"I consider the Puppet Master a friend at this point," I admitted.

"That's incredible. I'd love to talk to him," Tella gushed. "I haven't gotten the chance. Stabilizing the flora population has been my main goal lately."

"He's very friendly," I assured her. "I think he's lonely but he didn't realize it until he had other lifeforms to talk to."

"That's strangely sad," Tella frowned.

"I think so too."

"How come you haven't been working out of this lab?" Tella asked suddenly.

"I'm comfortable in my lab in Kaster," I answered but Tella narrowed her eyes.

"There's more to it than that."

Damn, she was good at reading people.

"The riots here lately have given me cause for

concern," I admitted. "Of course, a riot broke out in Kaster not long ago so the point seems moot."

"So, you haven't seen the lab we've got here?" A glimmer of excitement sparked in her eyes.

"Nope." A tingle of excitement spread through me. I may not have wanted to work in Nyhiem, but I'd only heard amazing things about the lab.

"Want to see it?"

"Do you even have to ask?"

Adam held up his hands. "I'm going to bow out of this field trip." He turned to me, giving me a fierce hug. "I'll catch you in a bit, alright?"

As he walked away, I had a flicker of worry, but then Tella tugged my arm.

"Come on!"

Tella and I sped off down the corridor. I wanted to giggle with excitement but I didn't want to look unprofessional.

The lab was better than anything I could've imagined. Pristine white walls, white floors, and white countertops lit up with blue consoles. Rows and rows of equipment, some of which I didn't even recognize.

"What's that?" I pointed excitedly at a dark metal machine that stuck out like a sore thumb.

"That's a chemical reconstructor," Tella explained. "It's really amazing. You can put in a decomposed organic material and it'll reconstruct a chemical profile with ninety-eight percent accuracy."

"That's incredible!" I gasped.

"The only thing it wasn't able to reconstruct was a chemical profile of the Puppet Master. We had to jigsaw that together ourselves."

"I wish I could've been here for that," I sighed.

"What were you doing before you were picked up by General Rouhr?"

"Monitoring Kaster's fish population, actually. The Xathi did a number on our planet. Most people think just the forests were affected but big disturbances affect the ocean too."

"And how's the fish population doing without you?"

"Thriving," I laughed dryly. "All they needed was an aqua-scrubber to get traces of the Xathi ship out of the area."

"Sounds riveting." Tella looked at me from the corner of her eye.

"I'm glad to be working with the Puppet Master, I'll tell you that much," I snorted.

I paused, feeling bad for joking about my job. I only had it because my mentor fell to the Xathi.

"Who's been running experiments on the Puppet Master's blood?" I asked.

"Is that what you call it?" Tella wrinkled her nose and laughed.

"Got anything better?"

"We've been calling it gloop."

"Oh, that sounds so much more professional," I chuckled.

"Times are tough. We have fun when we can," Tella shrugged. "Leena DeWitt and I have been working with your samples. We've found some incredible stuff in the gloop."

"Blood."

"Gloop."

"Neither are scientifically accurate," I laughed.

"But gloop is more fun to say."

"How have we not met sooner? I feel like we'd make good coworkers."

"Or friends," Tella grinned.

"Yes, or friends." I nodded.

"Come look at the lab results."

Tella lead me over to her console and pulled up several charts and spreadsheets.

"What do you see?" She asked.

"It's highly conductive," I observed. "How unusual."

"Yeah, Leena and I couldn't figure out why the Puppet Master would have something like this in his body. Thoughts?"

"Actually yes," I grinned. "Not long before I met Jalok, the Puppet Master explained to me that his lifeforce flowed like a river through the planet. What if this is part of the river?"

"I'm not sure I follow," Tella frowned.

"The Puppet Master told me every living thing on the planet drinks from his lifeforce river."

"Creepy."

"He phrased it better," I said dismissively. "We should test plants with signs of accelerated growth for traces of the blood-gloop. The Puppet Master could literally be secreting lifeforce, pushing more to areas that need more help regrowing." I snorted. "Although lifeforce might be an overly philosophical term for nutrients. He'll get a kick out of it."

"The Puppet Master likes philosophy?"

"That's kind of my fault," I winced. "I introduced him to the subject. He loves the mental stimulation."

"This just gets weirder and weirder."

"My best friend is a plant-god as old as the planet itself. Don't talk to me about weird," I laughed.

"Good point." Tella nodded. "Theoretically, the blood gloop is designed to help carry lifeforce throughout the planet. The lifeforce could be some kind of highly advanced plant food."

"Correct. Though I'd speculated the lifeforce is also something that helps him establish mental links to other creatures. Even creatures that don't have any mental capabilities."

"What are the odds of getting more lifeforce to run tests on?" Tella asked.

"I can always ask the Puppet Master," I reasoned. "It might not be something I can extract easily like I was able to extract the blood gloop."

"Let's say that lifeforce plus blood gloop equals controllable accelerated growth," Tella mused. "If we can crack that code, all we need is a Puppet Master-esque apparatus to spread the growth where we need it."

"That all sounds theoretically correct."

"Now we just need to make it realistically correct."

"You make it sound so easy," I laughed.

"I try." Tella paused and looked me over. "Want to go grab something to eat? I'm starving."

"Oh!" I lifted my brows in surprise. "That sounds nice but I'm actually going to meet up with my brother in a bit."

"Just a quick bite?" Tella sounded far too enthusiastic for someone I only met half an hour ago.

"Is there something I should know?" I asked.

Tella sighed and dropped her shoulders.

"Rokul should've never trusted me to do this," she tutted. "I'm not an actress."

"What are you talking about?"

"I honestly did want to talk to you about the Puppet Master and all that," she prefaced, "but the real reason I came up to you is because I'm supposed to keep an eye on you for the day."

"You could've just said that," I laughed. "It's fun having big alien bodyguards follow me everywhere but I'm glad to have some human companionship. Is Rokul off today or something?"

"Or something." Tella's smile looked unnatural.

"You really aren't an actress," I sighed. "What's happening? Is it something to do with Jalok?"

"No," Tella said quickly. "No, his recovery is going great from what I've heard. Rokul actually wanted to meet with your brother today."

"Adam didn't mention anything," I frowned.

"They're trying to keep it under wraps," Tella explained. "Rokul wants to get an idea of what's going on where Adam's been. Adam should know what's been happening outside of Duvest since that city is still rather isolated."

"Right," I said slowly, still trying to process the information I'd been given. "He still could've told me, though."

"Rokul probably told him not to," Tella said quickly. "Rokul tends to err on the side of over-caution. I think he loves the drama."

"He definitely has a flair for it," I chuckled.

"So, how about lunch?" Tella offered again.

"Sounds good." I mustered a smile and followed her out of the lab of my dreams.

I couldn't help but be disappointed that I wasn't getting to spend the afternoon with Adam.

But would be good for me to hang out with another human woman, particularly one who was in a relationship with a Skotan.

Maybe she could help me sort through my feelings.

Maybe.

JALOK

"**M**r. Jalok, please, will you get back to your bed?"
I couldn't blame the nurse on call for being upset.

After all, I was standing in front of her station, wearing a gown which opened up in back and revealed my rump to the world.

And I was surly as hell.

Not to mention the constant drip of fluid from the end of the intravenous line still partially attached to my arm.

This probably wasn't in her plan for the evening.

"Don't Mr. Jalok me, woman. I've had it with this place. You've done your job and healed me, now let me go and do mine."

The nurse pursed her lips, and took in my massive

form. She was probably calculating how many orderlies it would take to drag me back to my room by force.

In the end, she must have reached the only correct conclusion, which was there weren't enough orderlies in the entire hospital, and quite possibly the entire planet.

"Mr. Jalok, I don't have the authority to grant you a release. You have to speak to your attending physician first."

I cocked my head to the side.

"Okay, so who's my attending physician?"

"Just a moment, let me check." She started typing on her console, then frowned at my dripping tube. "Could you—could you pinch that off or something?"

"Sure." I ripped the tube right out of my arm, splashing a little blood on the floor. Those nurses are tough.

She didn't pass out at the sight, but at least she had the good grace to look disgusted. "There, fixed."

The nurse spoke on the comms for a moment while I waited impatiently. A few gawkers walked past me in the hall.

I made sure to smile toothily at them, and may even have flexed my scales to the surface a couple of times.

Just to entertain myself during the wait, of course.

"I'm sorry."

My gaze snapped back to the nurse.

"Sorry for what?"

"Your attending physician isn't on call today. He won't return until tomorrow, so you'll have to wait for your release until then."

"What? That's bullshit."

The nurse winced, and several patients and medical professionals gaped at my high volume.

"I'm sorry, I didn't mean to be that loud." I cleared my throat and spoke at a much lower volume. "That's bullshit. I'm ready to leave now."

"Be that as it may, sir, I can't authorize your release without his signature."

"So call him in."

"But it's his day off."

"He has a job to do."

"So do I. Please, return to your bed."

My hands clenched into fists, knuckles popping dramatically. I leaned over the desk and fixed her with a baleful gaze.

"Look, ma'am, let me ask you a question."

"Go on."

"Do you really want an angry, loud Skotan soldier here causing a disturbance for all of your other patients?"

She didn't have to consider that for long.

"No."

"Then how about we find a solution to our little problem?"

In short order, the nurse found a spare uniform that almost fit, and a physician on call who was willing to sign my release.

He gave me a long spiel about things I wasn't supposed to do, like eat large meals or go swimming.

Pretty standard stuff, and I tuned it all out. All I cared about was getting that stupid release so I could return to duty.

The truth was, I knew I was fine.

No pain, no tiredness, and the only issue I had was the itching on my arm. The doctor gave me a cream for the itch and signed my release, and away I went.

I was eager to get out of the damn hospital and back to duty, where I could be near Dottie again.

I hadn't been kept in the loop about her guard rotation. What if they weren't being vigilant enough?

A memory flashed through me, the feel of her naked, wet body.

What if they were trying to get to close?

I tried not to dwell on that particular thought.

Looking back, I could have called for an official transport, but that would have meant waiting longer.

At the hospital.

So I decided to walk instead back to base.

There was a lot of the city that's still being rebuilt

after the invasion, and like most dilapidated slums on any world you care to name there were undesirable elements who moved into such areas.

That wasn't much of a deterrence to me, however.

If I wanted to walk around the 'bad' part of the city, I would have to add two extra hours to my journey.

Not a thought I relished.

So I turned down the beaten up, cracked street and ignored the looming eyes which watched my progress intently.

Surely none of them would be dumb enough to pick a fight with an obvious soldier, especially not one of my size.

Of course, I wound up being wrong about that, too.

I realized I was being tailed after the first two blocks. Without being too obvious about it, I found a way to glance back the way I'd come and counted three humans in shabby clothing. They looked like they meant business, but I didn't feel any cause for alarm.

Then I strolled past a street corner where half a dozen more humans loitered. They stopped their conversation when I walked past, eyeing me intently.

I beamed them my widest smile and even waved.

If they were going to cause problems, maybe my nonchalance would throw them off and make them choose a different course of action.

After another block, however, it became obvious the

new group had joined my previous tail. They kept back behind me half a block away, but I was certain I was being stalked. To put my theory to the test, I took a left, then another left, and then a right at random. Sure enough, they continued to follow me without fail.

I decided at that point that there would be no way to avoid a confrontation.

As soon as they'd worked up their nerve, or decided I was too far away from the main thoroughfare for my cries for help to be heard, they would rush me.

But I turned the tables on them. I stopped in my path and bent over to check my perfectly tied boot laces. I hummed a little ditty while I waited for them to catch up.

They would either have to finally approach me closely, or walk past.

I waited until I heard their footsteps a dozen yards away and abruptly sprang up to a standing position. They blanched, exchanging worried glances as I flexed my scales to the surface.

In my best nonchalant tone, I spoke. "Are you boys lost?"

They again looked to each other in confusion. One of them, a bit bolder than the rest, stepped forward and shook his fist in the air.

"We don't want your kind here, alien scum."

"Yeah." One of his compatriots stepped forward to

stand abreast with him. "Look at what you've done to this city. To us. There's not enough to go around for us humans thanks to your alien greed."

"Wow, you boys have your talking points well-rehearsed." I cocked my head to the side and smiled. "But to be honest, you're boring the hell out of me. Can we just get to the part where you violently attack me so I can work out my frustrations?"

The two men glanced at each other. I could almost read their thoughts. *This isn't how this is supposed to go...*

"What, are you shy? Here, let me get you started."

I strode forward and snatched the first speaker up by his shirt collar. With one half assed toss, I could have shattered his spine against the nearby crumbling cement wall.

But then I remembered the horror on Dottie's face when I'd been wading into combat during the riot.

I just kind of slapped him against the wall instead, much more gently than I normally would. His head still bounced off hard, and his eyes went glassy. I dropped the man in a heap on the ground and grinned.

"Who's next?"

They surged forward, and I laid about myself with fists and feet.

Again, I pulled my punches because of Dottie.

She wasn't even there, and I was worried how she might react if I crippled or killed those men.

So I aimed my knuckles for their jaws, not their throats. When I had a hold of a miscreant by the throat, I just squeezed long enough for him to fall unconscious instead of snapping his neck like a twig.

And when they ran away—those that are still able—I just allowed them to leave.

I felt strange as I returned to my team.

Why did I care what Dottie felt about how I chose to defend myself? Why had I held back?

The answer never came to me.

When I got back to base, Sk'lar just rolled his eyes.

"If you're going to insist on being out of bed, back to bodyguard duty for you."

I tried to repress a grin. At that point, I had forgotten that it had even been intended as a punishment.

All I wanted was to get on the next shuttle for Kaster.

DOREK STOOD outside the apartment door, face blank. I clapped his shoulder and he narrowed his eyes. "You're relieved."

"Finally," he grumbled. "What a skrell assignment."

Good. He obviously hadn't gotten too close to Dottie.

She answered the door when I knocked. "You're back!" she squealed, and every moment of the day was worth it, just to have her near me again.

With a broad smile on her face, she flung her arms around my waist.

"Oh!" she scrambled back. "I'm sorry, you're still hurt."

I pulled her closer, just for a moment, just long enough to breath in her sweet scent. "I'm fine now, promise."

"Come in," she grabbed my hand and pulled me through the door. "You're just in time. They've just finished cooling!"

Inside the apartment, her brother stood in the kitchen, face carefully blank.

Dottie bustled around, cutting a large brown square into smaller squares, oblivious to his obvious displeasure.

"What's this?" I asked.

"These are brownies," she beamed at me.

"The ones that had been destroyed on your contraption?"

"Yes!"

She handed me the roughly cut brown cake and I placed it gingerly in my mouth.

The explosion of flavor lit my eyes.

"This is very good!" I exclaimed. "A warrior's food!"

"They're favorites of human children as well."

I laughed.

That evening, we talked, we laughed, and I found that, curiously enough, I couldn't seem to stop smiling in her vicinity.

But Adam stayed silent.

It seemed that being around Dottie again was the perfect balm for my aching sensibilities, which had been so mistreated during my hospital stay.

If only her brother hadn't been lurking about.

I wanted to trust Adam, but I couldn't shake the feeling that he just wasn't the benevolent guy he claimed to be.

From time to time I would catch him watching Dottie and I as we spoke.

There had been tightness, tension in his posture, and his cold gaze silently judged.

At the time, I tried to dismiss my feelings as mere paranoia, perhaps some left over apprehension from my near death experience.

So I made an effort to ignore his uneasy stares and enjoy my time with Dottie.

I was only partially successful.

DOTTIE

The knock at my bedroom door came an hour earlier than expected but I didn't mind. In fact, I was happy.

Jalok and I could have a bite of breakfast before heading into work. We were overdue for a relaxing morning.

"You're very early," I grinned when I opened the door. Jalok didn't smile back. In fact, he looked tense. "Is everything all right?"

"No," he sighed.

Panic rose in my throat. I inadvertently took a step back into my bedroom.

"What's wrong?" I could barely get the words out.

"You're going to have to stay home today," Jalok said gently.

"Someone else went crazy, didn't they? Who died? Is it Anita? Eluna?" My voice rose in pitch with each word and my hands started trembling.

"No one's dead." Jalok stepped close to me and lifted my wrists. He pressed my trembling hands together and wrapped his around. "Listen to me, no one is dead."

"Then what's wrong? Why do I have to stay here?"

"There's been a break-in at your lab," Jalok said.

"A break in?" Slowly, the words clicked into place. "What's been taken?"

"I'm not sure yet but whoever it was thoroughly trashed the place."

"The lab is under twenty-four-hour surveillance," I said. "Have whoever's looking into the break-in look through the footage."

"The cameras have been shut off for weeks," Jalok informed me.

"What? That's not possible. Highly classified work happens in that lab. There's no way it would be left unguarded."

"It's not uncommon for places with low funding to use cameras as a visual repellent rather than actual surveillance equipment," Jalok explained.

Oh.

He made a good point. Funding came in trickles rather than waves.

But to have cameras, and not really use them, seemed foolish.

"So, you have no idea what was taken or who did it?"

"Not at this time. The other members the Strike Team are working on it right now. They'll figure it out, I promise."

"All the more reason why I should be there!" I insisted. "I'm familiar with everything in my department. I can figure out what's been taken."

"That's out of the question."

"Why?" I demanded.

"You know why, Dottie. You're doing valuable work and under no circumstances are you to be put at risk."

"It's not my body that's valuable, it's the information I've gathered! Why can't I do my part in protecting that information?"

"Because if anything happens to your body, I'd lose my mind," Jalok exclaimed. "My job is to protect you. Please let me do that."

"It's not fair!" I couldn't hold back the floodgates on my anger any longer.

It all came pouring out of me. I started to pace the length of my living room, desperate to expel the frantic energy coursing through me.

"Fair?" Jalok blurted. "This issue is bigger than being fair."

"It's not fair that I'm not allowed to defend my life's work. It's not fair that I'm one of the only people who can figure out what's missing and you won't let me work! It's not fair that I can't get one single day without something going to shit!" I was shouting but I didn't care.

For the last few weeks, I've been keeping my mouth shut and doing what I needed to do.

How much more was I expected to put up with without batting an eye or losing my mind?

Tears welled up faster than I could blink them away. They spilled down my cheeks. When I tried to take a calming breath, sobs shuddered through my chest instead.

"Dottie?" Jalok's voice sounded so soft and caring. It only made the tears come faster.

"Leave me be for a minute, okay?" I couldn't look him in the eye. I felt like a child.

"No way." He closed the distance between us and placed his hands on my shoulders.

My eyes went to the burned, broken skin on his right arm. The sight of it only made me more upset. He only had those scars because he was assigned to protect me.

Unable to look at his scars, I stepped closer and put my head against his chest.

Jalok went stiff at first, then gently wrapped his arms around me.

"You're allowed to be upset over everything that's happened," he told me. "You've been through more than a normal person goes through in a lifetime."

"How do you know what a person goes through in a lifetime?" I asked.

"I don't. I was just trying to make you feel better. I pity you humans if your normal lives consist of this much change, stress, and violence."

I wasn't sure if he was joking or not, but I laughed anyway.

"I'm sorry for freaking out." I took a deep shuddering breath. "Between you getting hurt, my brother coming home, and now my work being trashed, I've hit every extreme emotion in a short time span. Most humans don't do well launching from one extreme to the other."

"Evidently. Come. Have a seat."

Jalok lead me over to the couch. Once I was settled, he sat down beside me and laid his hand on my back, rubbing in small circles.

"I'm fine now," I assured him.

"I'll ascertain that for myself, thank you."

I wanted to say something snarky in an attempt to bring us back to normal, but I couldn't make myself do it.

Instead, I took a deep breath and let my head rest against his shoulder. To my surprise, he rested his cheek on the top of my head.

I turned my head to look up at him and he leaned back to look at me.

"Are you all right?"

I didn't answer.

Instead, I leaned forward. My lips pressed against his in a gentle kiss.

When he didn't kiss me back right away, I felt embarrassed. I pulled away.

My cheeks burned red.

"I'm sorry," I blurted. "I wasn't thinking and-"

Jalok didn't let me finish. His hand snaked around my shoulder to the back of my neck. He pulled me to him and pressed his lips against mine, fiercely. Claiming me.

This time, I let myself sink into his kiss. I took in the warm, firm feeling of his lips.

His tongue flickered at the seam of my lips and I opened for him, letting his tongue twist around mine, in a prelude to what we both knew was coming.

He tasted like his scent. Warm, spicy.

Mine.

When we broke apart to catch our breaths, I searched his face. His eyes glimmered with a need that matched my own.

Fire raced through my veins and his hands, his touch, was the only thing that could quench the burning.

I kissed him again, harder, hungry.

Jalok's other hand pressed into the small of my back. When he pulled me as close as physically possible, I still felt the need to be closer.

Without breaking our kiss, I shifted so that I had one leg on each side of his lap. My chest pressed up against his. Something about that much physical contact with him at once ignited something in me.

I let out a soft, shuddering gasp when his large hand slipped under the hem of my tank top.

A cool breeze from the open window tickled my exposed skin and sent goosebumps up my spine. Jalok moved his hands up my back slowly.

I found myself arching against him, eager for his hands to explore more.

As if he read my mind, Jalok slipped my tank top towards my shoulders.

I raised my arms and allowed him to remove it completely.

When I lowered my hands, I tried to wrap them around his neck but he stopped me.

"Wait," he murmured. "I just want to look at you for a moment. The light's hitting your skin perfectly. You look like you're glowing."

I tipped my head back and basked in the warm morning light as Jalok ran his hands over my skin. A bolt of pleasure shot through me when I felt his hand on my bare breast.

He paused as if waiting to see if I'd pull away.

When I didn't, he started gently stroking his thumb over my nipple.

Sparks ran through me at his touch, driving me to move closer. As I rocked my hips, I felt the evidence of his arousal.

Oh.

He felt huge.

For a moment, panic ran through me. What was I doing?

Would this work? What if...

But desire pushed me along.

Only one way to find out.

I opened my eyes and reached for the clasp of his trousers. Just as I'd felt through the fabric, but now I could see him in his full, red, rigid glory.

And with every caress of his hands, down my back, around my thighs, over my breasts, I relaxed into him.

Wanted him more.

Jalok lifted me slightly so I could slip off the simple pair of navy panties I had worn to bed.

Naked in his arms, I leaned forward to kiss him again.

Jalok lifted my hips and slid forward. I spread my thighs for him. He lowered me slowly. When I felt him press against my entrance, I shuddered in anticipation.

Instead, Jalok teased me, just letting the broad head part my wet folds.

"You're cruel," I murmured.

"Only a little," Jalok smirked as he slowly lowered me onto him, controlling the agonizing, wonderful pace.

I let out a cry as our bodies joined together, as every thick, hard inch filled me, until finally, finally he was seated fully within.

"You're not the only one who can tease," I answered, working myself up and down the length of him, further stoking the heat that'd already built up inside me.

Jalok pressed his hands against my back, flattening me against him, taking back control. Every brush of my skin against his drove me closer to the edge. I threw my head back, urging him on with every rock of my hips.

When the pleasure inside me reached the point of no return, I sank my teeth into Jalok's shoulder. He let out a hiss and wound one of his hands into my hair.

I thought he was going to pull me back, but instead, he brought me closer, urging me to bite again.

Excited that I found something he liked, I left a trail of little bites from his shoulders up to his earlobe.

With a loud growl he tightened his grip on my

waist, burying himself deep inside me over and over again until I cried out, helpless against the wave of sensation slamming through me.

We reached our climax together.

At one point, we were so tightly wound together that I didn't know where my limbs ended and his began.

I slumped against his chest, spent and satisfied. Jalok held me close and pressed kisses into my hair.

"After all this," he murmured, "You deserve a lie in."

He scooped me up in his arms and carried me into the bedroom.

It was too hot for blankets so he laid me down on top of them.

After fetching a glass of cold water for each of us – I drank mine down in one go- he settled down next to me and held me as I drifted back to sleep.

The lab could wait.

Everything could wait.

He was beside me.

But even as I drifted away, content and lazy, I felt him pull away.

JALOK

Did I want to be skulking around after Adam as he meandered through the streets of Kaster that day?

Absolutely not.

What I wanted to do was bask in the afterglow of passion with Dottie.

Never in a million years did I believe I would be attracted to, let alone develop feelings for, a member of another species.

Humans are soft and squishy, and nowhere near as resilient as the Skotan are.

Not only that, they have the annoying habit of thinking they're right about everything.

But Dottie had challenged my prejudices, and made me second guess a lot of things about my life.

And I knew without a doubt, she'd be challenging me for years to come. I'd found my mate, and I planned to keep her.

The memory of her soft skin against mine lingered in my mind even as I tracked her brother.

Adam was allegedly going to have another meeting with the Search and Rescue unit in Kaster that day.

But Adam had been on his communicator.

A lot.

Far more than seemed necessary for someone as yet without a vocation or friends in the area.

It hadn't taken much convincing to get cousin Cazak to watch over Dottie for the rest of day.

Much as I wanted to spend my time with her, I couldn't let my suspicions about Adam go.

Tailing someone when you're built like I am is a daunting task. I didn't exactly blend into the crowd in Kaster, even though I was hardly the only Skotan around.

To make things more difficult, Adam was behaving strangely for someone allegedly on his way to a job interview.

He took a meandering, illogical path through the city.

After every half block he traversed, Adam would glance about himself as if suspicious of being followed.

Several times I was certain he was going to spot me,

but my hastily chosen cover protected me from his vision.

At one point, I was cowering behind a display of exotic shells from the nearby sea. The proprietor eyed me suspiciously with a narrowed gaze.

"What exactly do you think you're doing?"

"Official government business. Don't blow my cover."

"Half the people on the street can see you hiding behind my wares."

"I don't care about half the street.

I only care about one annoying human, and if your ceaseless prattle alerts him to my presence, I am going to be...perturbed."

I cracked my knuckles to reinforce my point.

The vendor blanched and then quickly turned his attention away from me, nervous sweat dripping down his brow.

Srell. That was the sort of thing that made Dottie grumpy.

I'd have to work on that.

Later.

I peeked through the legs of the vendor's stool, and saw Adam turn back and continue his haphazard journey.

"Thanks, citizen." I smiled toothily at the little human and then followed Adam. He turned around the corner at the next intersection and fell out of sight.

I counted ten of my own heart beats, then hurried to catch up.

Peering around the corner, I just caught a glimpse of him stepping over a safety barricade and heading down a street in too poor repair for common use. If I wasn't already suspicious, I certainly was now.

The Search and Rescue headquarters sat a half dozen blocks away, and he had no business whatsoever in that part of the still dilapidated town.

With Adam out of my sight, I bustled down to the alley. I didn't want to lose him in the labyrinthine corridors of the damaged block.

Still, I flattened myself to the wall and carefully peered around the corner, just in case he was close.

Adam had stopped a half block into the alley. He walked up to a metal door and rapped.

After a few tense moments, the door swung open and a scruffy looking human emerged, wearing no shirt but a rubber apron and matching gloves.

Exactly the type of gear one would wear, say, if one were building homemade gas bombs like the ones used in the riot.

The scruffy man was known to me because of my myriad debriefings after the Kaster riot.

He was believed to be the leader of the Kaster anti-alien cell, Jaxon Wolfe. Wolfe was seen on surveillance footage of the riot organizing the most violent sects of the anti-alien protesters.

However, he was not caught overtly committing acts of violence himself, which made procuring a warrant for his arrest tricky, even if his location could be pinned down.

Wolfe took off his gloves and shook Adam's hand. Both men had big smiles on their faces.

In my years as a soldier, I've found that no one has a grin quite like someone dedicated to an irrational belief system.

They smile like that because they think they have it all figured out. Life, the Universe, and everything all wrapped up in their neat little ideology.

In this case, however, their ideology was centered around the right of myself and other aliens to live and breathe. I couldn't help but take it personally.

They were too away for me to make out what they're saying, and I couldn't read lips in Skotan, let alone the human tongue.

Their smiles faded as the discussion turned serious. Wolfe did most of the talking, while Adam nodded in agreement.

Were they planning an act of terror against the alien citizens, or were they just talking about what was for dinner?

Unfortunately, I had no way to tell.

But it was a safe bet that they were discussing dark subjects. The two men talked for some time, the shadows stretching out longer as the sun drifted across the sky.

From time to time they would smile or even laugh, but for the most part their discussion appeared quite grim from my admittedly limited perception.

Adam and Wolfe shook hands once more, and then embraced one another. Wolfe held Adam by the shoulders at arm's length and spoke to him solemnly.

Whatever he said had quite an effect on Adam.

Dottie's brother appeared stunned, but then he gave Wolfe a curt nod.

The two men finished their meeting, with Wolfe retreating back into the door he'd come from. I made a mental note of where to find it.

Adam turned and started walking back toward the main street, and I hastily struggled to find cover.

I found a spot behind an overflowing trash bin, but when my great weight settled against the hot metal side I dislodged a food can. With despair, I watched it clank down onto the deserted street.

Cursing silently, I squeezed myself against the wall. There was enough of a gap between the bin and the building next to it that I could see Adam step out from the alley. He peered suspiciously in my direction.

Then he moved out of my sight. I waited for tense moments, expecting him to pop out into view and find me at any second.

Then I started thinking, why was I even hiding anymore? I wasn't the one meeting with a suspected terrorist, after all. I wasn't the one acting suspiciously.

I decided I would simply confront Adam then and there.

Boldly, I stepped into the street, expecting to see Adam almost on top of me. Instead, I was greeted by an empty road.

"Shit."

I took off at a dead run, heading back for the last cross street. When I reached the corner, I saw the vendor with his sea shells, and myriad other folk going about their business, but there was no sign of Dottie's brother.

Frantically, I retraced our weird, illogical route, but still found no sign of Adam.

Apparently my noise had made him even more paranoid, or he'd always intended to take a different route back home.

Home. He wouldn't be heading home. He'd be headed for Dottie's.

I now knew what I had to do. Giving up my fruitless search for Adam, I instead made haste for Dottie's flat.

I had a terrible feeling, and more than anything

wished could have called up central command for a rift, but of course Fen had put the nix on all rift travel for the time being.

My recent stay in the hospital still haunted me, as I was far too winded for such a trivial amount of exertion when I reached Dottie's.

But the feeling wouldn't let me rest.

What if something happened to her? I took the stairs two at a time. When I reached her apartment, I didn't bother to knock or use the door chime. I just burst right on in.

Three pairs of eyes snapped over to me as I stumbled inside, panting from fatigue.

Dottie and Adam stood in the kitchenette, making lunch, while my cousin Cazak sat nearby with a datapad in his hand.

"Jalok, what's wrong?" He asked the question in a way that let me know he knew what was up, but was putting on a show for Dottie's benefit.

"You look awful." Dottie quickly poured me a glass of water, but I didn't take the offered vessel.

Instead I glared at Adam.

"Maybe Adam should tell you what's wrong."

His eyes narrowed, but a smile played at his lips.

"I have no idea what you're going on about, Skotan."

"Really?" I jabbed my finger in his direction. "So you

just weren't meeting with a suspected anti-alien terrorist?"

Panic flashed over Adam's face, quickly replaced with faux indignation.

"How dare you make such an accusation. I've been meeting with Search and Rescue all day."

"You lie."

"Be careful what you say, scaly." Adam sneered. "I'm not afraid of you, and I don't take kindly to being falsely accused."

I snarled, and took a step toward Adam, but Cazak stepped between us.

"I'll solve this little problem. Let's just give Search and Rescue a call and confirm Adam's alibi."

Adam shook with rage as Cazak made the call, and I awaited validation with a knowing smile.

Foolish human. He should have known not to fight me, even if this wasn't a traditional battlefield.

But as I realized it would break Dottie's heart, my victory turned to ashes in my mouth.

DOTTIE

"Jalok, is this really necessary?" I demanded.

"I'm sorry, Dottie." His tone changed from harsh and accusatory into the gentle voice I'd become accustomed to hearing. "You know I wouldn't do this unless I felt I had to."

I searched Jalok's expression and found nothing but open honesty in his eyes.

I wish that made me feel better.

I looked at Adam, who shot me a pleading gaze.

"Dottie, this is ridiculous and you know it. They're all paranoid. Who could blame them for it?" He gestured to the others in the room. "But you know me better than anyone. You know how much I've done for Search and Rescue. Why would I jeopardize that?"

I stood between my brother and the alien I thought I was falling in love with.

I looked from one to the other, unsure what I was supposed to do in this situation.

"I'm calling to confirm the location of one of your team members," Cazak spoke into the receiver.

Adam turned a shade paler. I knew before Cazak disconnected that Adam lied to us.

Tears filled my eyes. I blinked them away even though it hurt to do so.

"Thank you for the information." Cazak disconnected and gave Jalok a nod. "You were right. The Search and Rescue team hasn't heard from Adam in a few days. They're under the impression he took time off to visit his sister."

"You used me?" My voice sounded dry and pinched, nothing like my own. Jalok reached out for me but I put up a hand to stop him. I was too angry to be touched right now.

"Dottie, you don't get it," Adam groaned.

"Then explain it to me," I said through gritted teeth.

"I came here to meet with a notable leader of the Pro-Human Coalition," Adam explained.

"Have you lost your goddamned mind?" I yelled.

"Have you?" Adam bellowed back.

"Watch it," Jalok threatened. He moved closer to me. This time, I didn't stop him.

"Shut up, scum."

"Adam!" I hissed.

Cazak put his hand on the hilt of his weapon. I lifted my hand, silently pleading with him not to draw it.

"I came here to talk to them so that I could ensure your safety," Adam said to me.

"My safety?" I sputtered. "I'm as safe as I'm going to get!" I gestured to the two armed aliens in the room.

"I refuse to believe you're that naïve," Adam scoffed. "The aliens don't want to help us. They want to rule over us."

"That's simply not true."

"Of course, is it." Adam wound his fingers into his hair. "I don't want them dead. I swear, I'm not like those other terrorists that want to slaughter them all. I'm not like that!"

"Then why are you seeking them out?"

"The leader I met with has a brilliant plan."

"Did Jaxon Wolfe start the riot in Kaster?" Jalok demanded.

"He never told me," Adam smirked. "Even if I knew, I wouldn't tell you."

"We have ways of getting the information we want." Cazak cracked his knuckles.

"He said he doesn't know," I repeated.

"How can you believe anything he says after this?" Cazak demanded.

"Because he's family. Let him speak."

"Thank you, little sister," Adam smiled. "The man I met with doesn't want to kill all of the aliens either. He's just like me!"

There was a crazed gleam in Adam's eyes. It broke my heart. This couldn't be happening. I'd just gotten my brother back, and now I was going to lose him.

"What does he want, then?"

"Like me, he realizes that there are benefits to having them around. They have better tech, better resources. They can help us fix the planet."

"Finally, he says something that makes sense," Jalok mumbled. I nudged his side gently, urging him to be quiet.

"How is he anti-alien if he believes that?" I prompted. "That doesn't sound like a terrorist at all."

"His plan is to allow the aliens to fix up our planet then force them out. The aliens don't want to be here either! They have their own home planets. It's a win-win situation!"

That didn't exactly make sense. From what I'd heard, the aliens couldn't go home if they wanted. They were stuck here.

But I needed to keep Adam talking.

The more information he spilled, the more useful it'll be to Jalok and Cazak.

"What about the aliens who've found mates here?" I prompted.

Adam's expression soured. "Mates," he spat. "The aliens didn't find mates. They found toys."

"Some human women have already married their alien soulmates," I reminded him, thinking of the smile on Tella's face. She'd never be anyone's toy, that was for certain.

"Oh yes," Adam nodded. "I saw that story on the news about a human woman giving birth to a little hybrid monster. Disgusting. That creature is an abomination. It's directly defiant of humanity. It should be drowned or shot into space."

"Adam!" I gasped. "You don't mean that. What happened to not wanting to kill the aliens?"

"I don't want them here. I want them gone," he snapped. "If that can be achieved without killing, that's fine. If it can't, I'm willing to do what's necessary. That hybrid creature cannot be allowed to grow up here. This planet is not its home."

"Don't you see that the aliens have kept me safe? They've become my friends."

"Oh, they've become much more than your friends," Adam sneered. "Did you think I wouldn't see it? You and him." Adam looked past me and glared at Jalok.

"He's saved my life on several occasions. One of those occasions was when a radical tried to kill me."

"You're falling for it, Dottie! You can't even see it!" Adam shrieked. "He's going to make you into a breeder just like that other woman! I won't ever let that happen to my little sister."

I stepped back, shocked, as white hot rage poured through me.

"I should slap you for that," I hissed. "You don't get to say things like that to me. I've been on my own for a long time, Adam. That's partially because you never thought to let me know you're alive. You seemed to think I was perfectly capable of handling myself then, and I'm perfectly capable now. I don't need you to look out for me especially, if you're going to do it like this."

"If you're going to be this stupid, then you deserve whatever comes to you." Adam stormed out of the living room and into my bedroom. He slammed the door with enough force to rattle the light fixtures.

"That's my room, asshole!" I shouted, then sagged against the wall.

Cazak, Jalok and I stood in tense silence.

"I could arrest him if you want," Cazak suggested. "Get him out of here."

"No," Jalok and I said at the same time. I looked at him in surprise.

"If we leave him free but monitor him, we can figure out who he's been talking to," Jalok suggested. "We know to an extent now, but we can work further down the terrorist cell. It's what got us this far."

"I'm not exactly thrilled with how far you've got," I snapped.

Jalok looked at me in surprise.

"It's getting late," Cazak said quickly. "I'm going to head back to Command."

"He'll be right behind you." I threw a pointed look at Jalok.

"No, I will not," Jalok protested.

Cazak took the opportunity to sneak out the front door.

"I don't want you and Adam in the same apartment." I explained. "You two are like oil and water."

"I'm not going to leave you alone here with Adam," Jalok insisted, jaw set. "Did you hear anything he said? He's losing his mind!"

"Don't talk about my brother that way," I hissed. "I agree with you that something's wrong but he's still my family."

"I understand that but he's been associating with anti-alien radicals!"

"I know!" I groaned. "I wish I didn't know!"

"You'd rather be in danger and not know about it?"

"No." I pressed the back of my hand into my forehead as if it would stop the oncoming headache. "I'm sorry," I sighed.

"I'm just trying to do my job and keep you safe," Jalok said gently. "I can't let anything happen to you."

"I know. I just," tears welled up in my eyes again. I let a few escape and slide down my cheeks. "I just got Adam back. Now I feel like I'm losing him all over again."

"I know." Jalok took a step closer to me but I backed away. "Are you angry with me?"

"I'm angry at everything right now," I told him.

The truth was that I felt anger towards him.

He was the one who revealed Adam's liaison in the first place. If Jalok hadn't been so determined, I'd still have my older brother.

Or at least, the illusion of him.

I knew my train of thought made no sense. I knew it wasn't fair. But I also knew that I needed to be angry.

I couldn't bring myself to be angry at Adam yet. There was some kind of blockage stopping me from despising him like I should.

I felt like a monster as I sat down on the couch with my back to Jalok.

"You don't have to talk to me about it now," he said after a long silence. "But we are going to talk about it. And I'm not leaving you here alone. I'll sleep on the floor if I have to. Not sure the couch can take much more."

Anger forced me to choke on my words. I wanted to

tell Jalok how much I appreciated him and that I didn't blame him for anything.

But I couldn't make the words come. They were trapped in a cloud of irrational, seething anger. They'd stay that way until I had time to sort through my thoughts.

More than anything, I wished I could talk to the Puppet Master.

But there was no way Jalok would let me go to visit him in the middle of the night.

Instead, I curled up in the corner of the couch and did everything I could not to scream.

JALOK

My eyes snapped open in the shrouded dark of Dottie's living space. I hadn't been sleeping well ever since the chemical attack, and the slightest thing could awaken me.

In this case, it was some furtive movement from Dottie's kitchen. I knew her movements, her footsteps. But now, the shuffling stride alerted me to the fact that the source was none other than Adam.

For a time, I considered returning to sleep. He was staying there after all, and despite my misgivings toward him—and his ill feelings toward me—he had yet to do anything overtly violent.

But my inability to slumber deeply meant that I was fully awake. Realizing that I would likely have to wind back down before I could return to sleep, I decided to wait him out.

Surely he would finish his business in the kitchen soon enough. At the time I figured that it would be better if we just didn't cross paths in the late night hour.

So I laid there, perfectly still and silent, and waited for Adam to complete his task, whatever it may have been. Shuffle shuffle.

Rattle. The distinct sounds of a drawer being opened and someone rummaging around inside. From the metallic clinks, I believed Adam was digging about the knife drawer.

My heart started beating faster. I tried to calm myself down. Adam, for all I knew, might have been preparing a midnight snack for himself.

Completely innocuous and innocent.

But I couldn't shake the feeling that there was something amiss.

I waited, silently, only the sound of my own heart pounding in my ears. If he were preparing a meal for himself, he would soon have to open the refrigeration unit.

Not that Dottie really kept much in there.

Still, there came no sounds of the fridge door opening, and now I was convinced that my gut instinct was correct.

Carefully, I reached up and unsnapped my knife from its sheath.

The knife handle felt good and reassuring in my hand.

Now I waited again, this time alert for any sign of danger. Adam's shuffling steps approached, then halted.

"You know, I've always looked out for my sister."

In the gloom, I couldn't make out exactly where Adam was, but I could hear his voice coming from the direction of the kitchen.

His voice seemed oddly stilted, as if he were speaking carefully from a script.

"Ever since we were little kids, it was me who was there for her. When someone pushed her down at the park, I was right there. If some jerk-off tried getting too friendly, I was there, too. You see, I won't let anything bad happen to Dottie."

There was a definite undercurrent of threat in his tone.

I've heard people try to talk themselves up into doing something stupid before, but this sounded different. Far too calm under the circumstances.

"Dottie is special. But she's too nice. She's too nice to people who are far more dangerous than she realizes. If she gets hurt by the alien assholes who fucked up our planet, well, those assholes...those assholes are going to *pay.*"

I remember thinking, 'this is it.'

I'm going to have to kill Dottie's brother.

And I'll lose her forever.

That's when the light suddenly switched on. Blinking in the sudden brightness, I saw Adam several paces away, brandishing a kitchen knife. When the light came on, I had rolled out of the couch and to my feet, my own weapon held at the ready.

Dottie stood near the hallway, her eyes still puffy and bleary with sleep, hand on the light control panel.

But her stark gaze was fully awake as she took in the sight of Adam and I a few feet away, apparently about to get into a knife fight.

"What in the world is going on?"

She turned her gaze from me to her brother, demanding an answer from one or both of us. I opened my mouth to respond, but the sight of Adam gave me pause.

He was sweating profusely, and his stark gaze had a surreal, unsettling shine about it.

With a guttural growl, Adam leaped forward, plunging the knife toward me in a downward arc.

I used my own blade to parry the strike, knocking his knife far out to the side. If I had wanted to, I could have struck while his guard was broken.

One upward slice and I'd have buried my blade to

the hilt in his abdomen, reaching up through his rib cage to find the vulnerable heart.

But I didn't want to kill Dottie's brother—particularly not right in front of her.

So I didn't complete the strike. Instead, I lifted my leg up to hip level and thrust out with a potent kick.

Adam took the blow in his solar plexus and sprawled backward. His face didn't contort with pain, and he barely even grunted.

And through it all, his eyes maintained that same glossy, almost psychotic focus.

He lifted himself from the ground, a sprawling mass of sinew and limbs, and launched himself at me again.

Dottie's scream echoed off the walls as he attacked anew. "Adam, stop. What are you doing?"

I barely avoided his whirring blade. He thrust high, and I ducked underneath. He thrust low, and I leaped into the air, my head brushing the ceiling.

And through it all, I passed up a half dozen opportunities to bury my own knife in his soft tissue.

"Listen to your sister." That was all I managed to get out between wildly dodging for my life. My scales popped to the surface, and for the first time that frightened Dottie.

"Jalok, don't hurt him. Please."

Easy for her to say, while he was trying to stick me with his knife.

I parried another blow, and my arm vibrated from the impact.

It seemed impossible that his spindly body could generate that much force. Despite my Skotan heritage, I found that Adam was driving me back.

I back pedaled a few more steps until I wound up flush with the wall. Adam continued his assault, oddly silent except for gasps and grunts of exertion.

Somehow it was more unsettling than his previous threats.

Then it all went to hell.

My foot got entangled with a power cord and I was unable to stop Adam's thrusting attack. I could only watch and hope my scales absorbed the brunt of the impact.

I hissed as his blade slid along my abdomen, but despite a flash of pain his knife failed to penetrate.

Still, the attack had nearly succeeded, and it changed my tactics.

I still didn't want to kill Adam.

But neither could I allow him to kill me.

My stance changed. I lowered myself closer to the floor, presented half of my body as a target, and held the knife behind me with the blade reversed.

Adam came at me, slashing down at my head with a speed that belied his humanity. I brought my own knife upward, and the two blades collided.

There was a grating, gnashing sound which set my teeth on edge. Sparks flew from our blades as they ground against each other.

I couldn't believe how strong Adam was.

He slapped both of his hands onto the hilt of his blade and tried to push me backward. That's what I had been waiting for.

I stepped into his body, pivoted on my lead foot, and slammed my hip into his midsection.

With a twisting motion, I hurled him over my shoulder to land hard against the floor. The knife in his hands went bouncing away, but I had to make sure he would no longer be a threat.

I brought my hand down in a chopping motion, but I aimed for his temple instead of his throat. My scaled fist cracked against his nose, and Adam's head lolled to the side.

His eyes lost the unusual shine, and then closed.

"Oh my god." Dottie kneeled next to her brother and placed her fingers on his neck. She sighed with relief. "He's still alive."

"Of course he is. I'm a professional. And you don't like it when I kill people."

I snagged my comm off the coffee table and called for backup.

Despite the late hour, I was answered almost

immediately. I explained the situation and sat down on the sofa, holding my head in my hands.

Dottie picked up the knife her brother had used and threw it out the window.

Not exactly protocol, but I had to admit it was out of his reach that way. I expected civilian security to arrive quite soon.

"Why were you fighting? What happened?"

"I don't know." I sighed, feeling all of the fatigue from my lingering injuries. "I don't know, Dottie."

We both started when a knock came at the door. I stood up and answered, and was shocked to find both cousin Cazak and Rokul there, along with Tella.

They entered the apartment and stared down at Adam's unconscious form.

"Is he...?"

I shook my head.

"No, he's alive."

Dottie rambled, talking a mile a minute as she struggled to take in the situation. Fortunately, Tella took her gently by the hand and led her a few steps away, murmuring softly the whole time.

I was left with my cousin, Rokul, an unconscious anti-alien bigot, and a whole lot of questions.

DOTTIE

"Can't you go one day without getting into some kind of srell, Jalok?"

Cazak spread his arms out wide, gaze narrowed as he tried to stare down his cousin.

Difficult given Jalok's size, but he was trying.

I was afraid of what might happen. The horrid sight of my brother and the huge, scaled Jalok fighting with knives had emblazoned itself in my mind.

No matter what I looked at, or what was said, I only heard and saw superficially.

"It wasn't my fault." Jalok stared down at him and sneered. "I'm fine, by the way, thanks for asking."

"Hanging around humans has made you soft."

"Maybe. I was soft enough to take him out without seriously hurting him."

"Gentlemen." Tella pushed the two Skotan apart and gave them both a glare. Though both aliens dwarfed the scarred woman, they gave ground before those fierce eyes. "You're upsetting Dottie."

Jalok looked my way, his face a wreck of conflicting emotions.

On the one hand, he seemed to want to comfort me, but on the other he knew he had just nearly killed my brother. I didn't know what to think in that moment, so I turned my face away from him.

Tella took me by the shoulders and firmly steered me back into my bedroom. My legs were like rubber, barely able to hold me up. It seemed as if no matter how much air I sucked into my lungs, I still couldn't breathe. Drowning on dry land.

"Sit." Tella guided me to my bed and I obligingly sat down on the mattress. She knelt down before me, giving me the once over, and then reached into her boot and withdrew a metal flask. "Drink."

I turned my face away from the proffered stainless steel nozzle and protested.

"Drink." She spoke more firmly, and I accepted the flask.

Whatever was inside burned all the way down, but I found it easier to breathe. Tella took the flask back, stared at it a moment, then shrugged and took a pull herself.

Outside of my room, I could hear Jalok talking to Rokul and Cazak.

I didn't want to hear it, but I had to know.

What had happened?

"Want to go over that one more time, cousin?" Cazak's voice wasn't even muffled by the thin walls.

"I told you, I knew he was going to attack me because the fridge never opened—"

"That's an assumption. What evidence do you have to back that up?"

I heard a sharp intake of breath from Jalok. "What's that supposed to mean? Whose side are you on?"

"I'm just saying, this is how it's going to break down if there's an investigation into this. You have to be prepared if this goes sour, Cousin."

"How could it go sour? He attacked me."

"You had stated you'd already drawn your knife at this point. How do you know he wasn't just afraid you were going to assault him and panicked?"

"The lights weren't even on then. Can humans see in the dark? He had no way of knowing I even had it out."

"Well, you have me there. What happened then?"

"Dottie turned the lights on, and he went berserk. He got me a couple times with the knife, but it didn't penetrate my scales. I took him down using nonlethal means. I called you right after. That's all there is to it."

I turned away, unable to even process any of it.

Adam had attacked Jalok? In the dark? With a knife?

Tella sat down beside me on the bed.

"How you holding up, kid?"

"My brother just tried to kill my…" I swallowed hard. That was a level of complication I couldn't even deal with right now. "… bodyguard. Right in front of me. How do you think I feel?"

Tella shrugged.

"I think you probably feel like shit, to begin with. I think you might also feel overwhelmed and are on the verge of shock, so you need to calm down for me, all right?"

I remember thinking, it was easy for her to say that. I tried to take her advice, and focused on slowing my breathing.

My head still swirled with overwhelming notions, but at least my heart wasn't about to explode.

"What's really messed up is that Jalok is the one who found Adam for me in the first place. I thought maybe they could be friends. But Adam was suspicious from the start."

Something occurred to me, something I hadn't really had time to digest.

"Why did Jalok help find Adam originally? It didn't gain him anything," I asked.

"Hmm." Tella fought, and lost a battle to keep a

smirk off her scarred face. "Well, why did he? Why do you think he would do that?"

She turned it around on me. But as I considered the possibilities, none of them made any sense. Except one.

Oh.

"He did it to make me happy."

Tella chuckled.

"Does that help you process this whole, ah, mess better?"

"Not really." I sighed, and pulled my knees up to my chest. I rested my chin on my kneecaps and rocked myself slowly. "It's all so messed up. Why does it have to be happening like this? Why would my brother try to kill the man who reunited us after so long? Why did the two men I care about the most have to engage in mortal combat right in my living room?"

My erstwhile counselor patted me on the shoulder and nodded sagely.

"So you do care about Jalok. Are you sure you two aren't a thing?"

"I—" My mouth hung open, and I couldn't make myself deny it.

I did care about Jalok. Despite him being a huge jerk a lot of the time, and being in need of a serious attitude adjustment, he was a good man. Good alien.

And the things he'd done with my body, that loving, passionate touch…

"Jalok has a good heart."

Tella smiled, and stood up.

"That's true."

"It is true. But—what do I do with all of this, this mess? I'm so confused. I know Adam doesn't like the *Vengeance* crew, but he would never have taken things this far before. I love Adam, but now I'm a little bit afraid of him."

"I wish there was something I could say to make it better. You're in a tough spot, but maybe there's an explanation for what he did. Don't write him, or Jalok, off just yet."

I stood up as well, and crossed my arms over my chest.

"Who said I was giving up on either one of them? I just want this nightmare to be over. I'm only human, okay? I'm not some big shot hero like you."

Her face twisted into a sardonic grin.

"I'm no hero, Dottie. No one really is. All we can do is act when destiny calls upon us. The ones that succeed get saddled with the hero bullshit. The ones that don't, well, are they any less valid? A lot of folks have died, in the Xathi invasion and just trying to coexist on this planet. Nobody died tonight. Maybe you should focus on that, before you start to panic. Adam is alive, and Jalok is too. You didn't lose either of them."

That's when I realized what was happening. During

the Xathi invasion, when I thought I'd lost Adam, there had been a profound sense of emptiness.

Then I got him back, and that void had been somewhat filled. Nothing could make up for the time he had been missing, but just having him close again had been fulfilling.

Then, when I saw the two men I loved the most fighting each other, that yawning chasm of loss loomed before me again.

It was as if I'd been shoved up to the precipice of a deadly fall and hadn't quite convinced myself I was safe.

Suddenly I felt dizzy once more. I swooned, then collapsed onto my rump on the bed.

"Oh god." I hung my head in my hands, shoulders shaking with sobs. Tella sat down next to me and put her hand on my shoulders.

"Hey, it's all right. Just let it out."

I cried for some time, until my face swelled up and I could barely breathe through my nose.

Through it all, Tella just sat there next to me, providing comfort without any obligation, allowing me to vent my feelings without judgement.

A commotion in the living room drew me from my reverie. I wiped my face on the handkerchief given me by Tella, and opened the door.

A group of first responders had arrived. They were

taking Adam's vital signs, and preparing to load him onto a waiting gurney.

"Hey, take good care of him, all right? He's—" Jalok sighed, and shook his head. "He's important to somebody important to me, get it?"

"He'll be in good hands." The technician smiled up at Jalok with the patience of a saint. I guess one needs to have that sort of feckless aplomb in her line of work.

I watched as my unconscious brother was loaded onto the gurney.

Tears flowed from my eyes again when Cazak slapped a metal manacle on his ankle and then snapped the other cuff to the support struts of the gurney.

Then I stood while Adam was wheeled away, and I couldn't stand it anymore. I rushed back to my room, shut the door, and sat in silent misery.

JALOK

The sound of my heavy boots thunking on the tiled floor of the detention center echoed off the plain, reinforced walls. I was accosted several times and asked to show my identification and credentials.

Security was tight, and not just because Adam was a violent offender. Brass was worried, and for that matter so was I.

Four days had passed since Dottie's brother Adam attacked me in her apartment. Every single one of them I stopped by the detention center to visit him.

At first the guards assumed I was up to some sort of lame attempt at revenge. They separated us by a glass wall and refused to allow us in the same room.

On the third day they finally put us across from

each other at a table, albeit while two wary guards kept a close watch.

At that point, I was already convinced of my theory.

I had come to suspect that Adam may not have been in his right mind.

When I visited, I always asked him to recount his version of events on that fateful evening.

This is a common tactic in questioning a suspect, because you want to make certain the perp's story stays consistent. If he deviates from his original narrative, it's most likely because he was lying one or both times.

Adam, however, remained consistent throughout each retelling of his story. I flashed my credentials for the final checkpoint, then endured a pat down by a K'ver guard before being ushered into the plain, spartan room where I would have discourse with Adam.

He sat there in his seat that day, shoulders slumped and face drawn with weariness. The manacles connecting his wrists by a short length of chain were unnecessary. He was a defeated man, and was more troubled by his violent attack than even I was. Though perhaps not more troubled than Dottie.

The event had traumatized her to the core.

Adam sighed when I sat down opposite him. I'm certain he was weary of speaking about the traumatic night, but if I didn't need answers so badly I wouldn't make him go through it all over again.

"I've already told you everything, Jalok." He held his head in his hands and sank further into himself. "What's the point of doing it again?"

"Just once more, please. Indulge me."

Using manners instead of bullying my way through was something I'd picked up from hanging around Dottie.

Maybe she was rubbing off on me more than I'd thought.

"All right, fine." He looked up and flashed me a weak smile, though his eyes remained haunted. They didn't have that glossy madness of that night, thought. "I did try to kill you. I suppose going through it one more time is a small recompense."

"Then start at the beginning. When you first awakened, did you feel strange or emotional in any way?"

"No, I only felt hungry." He laughed softly, but the hard sardonic edge was directed at himself. "I really did go to get a sandwich or something."

"Walk me through it, please. You headed out of the bedroom, and then what? Step by step."

Adam's brow furrowed as he gathered his thoughts.

"Well, I walked into the kitchen, it was really dark. I didn't want to wake....well, I didn't want to wake you up. I just didn't want another argument, I just wanted to eat."

"So you didn't want to argue. It was dark, and then?"

"Then I went to the counter, I opened the drawer and I got out the knife. I was going to carve out some of that roast left from dinner the other night. But then, I-- it was like I was watching my body move on its own, like I was being... being pushed."

"So you never harbored any anti-alien resentment?"

Adam laughed, and leaned back in his chair.

"Of course I did. I've never been a fan of the *Vengeance* aliens. I mean, you brought your war down upon us. Lots of us died. But as much as I might vote for the anti-alien candidate, maybe even participate in a protest or two, I've never been violent about it."

"You were pushed to say things you didn't mean?"

"No, that's not it at all. I meant what I said. It was my feelings, but not my actions. I don't know what else I can tell you."

He sank his head to the table and seemed deflated.

I stood up and nodded to the guard to indicate I was ready to leave. "That's all for today, Adam. Thanks again."

To clear my head, and maybe clear the air, I headed toward Dottie's place.

I hadn't been there since the fight, knowing she needed the space. Others had taken temporary guard duty, and I knew she was safe.

At least physically.

But I didn't know how things stood between us, and I needed her, like the air in my lungs. Maybe more so.

Every step taunted me. Will she want me? Will she, won't she, will she.

For the first time, my knock was tentative. Maybe it would have been better to give her more time, maybe …

Then the door opened, and Dottie stood there in the doorway, all soft loveliness. For a time we stared at each other, and I feared it was anger that shone in her eyes.

Then she wrapped her arms around me and we held each other for a bit.

It was hardly a lover's passionate kiss, but having her near me was all I needed.

"Come in," she said softly, weaving her tiny fingers through mine.

We sat on the sofa holding cups of tea we had no interest in drinking.

"Listen, I, ah," I tried to start. "I'm not angry at Adam any more. I don't think he was responsible for his actions."

She smiled up at me and took one of my hands in both of her own. "I know."

"What? You do?"

"I haven't been just moping around for the past four

days, you know. I've been speaking a lot with the Puppet Master. At the exact moment of Adam's berserker rage, the Puppet Master sensed a sort of signature he hadn't felt in a millennia. He also felt it when Dyrn attacked me. Adam wasn't in his right mind, not one bit."

Sitting there holding her hand, I felt a surge of emotion. After all we'd been through I didn't want there to be any murkiness between us.

"Dottie, listen, I, that is, I wanted to say that..." Srell. Why couldn't this be as easy as combat? How would she even react to the word 'mate' after what her brother threw in her face?" "I really--I really like being with you."

Her face lit up and she squeezed my hands. "Really? What makes you say that?"

"Well, I guess you make me feel like maybe I can belong here, even if it's not the Skotan homeworld. Maybe it can still be my home."

She smiled, and kissed the back of my hand.

"I like being with you, as well. Even though you can act like a violent thug, I feel perfectly safe around you. You have a good heart, Jalok. I'd love for us to prove that human alien relationships can work."

"I can think of one way to prove it," I murmured, pulling her towards me.

She giggled and put down her teacup on the coffee

table. "And what would that be," she smiled. "Speaking as a scientist."

I kissed the soft curve of her neck, savoring the taste of her skin. "We'll have to make up experiments as we go along."

She melted into me and I couldn't take it anymore, couldn't keep up the laughing and joking persona.

I needed her. Needed her now. Needed her forever.

"Dottie," I ground out and thankfully she knew everything I meant in that one word.

Perfect mate.

"Yes," she breathed, winding her arms around my neck. "Yes."

I scooped her into my arms and brought her back to the bedroom. "First thing tomorrow I'm getting you a new couch," I growled.

Then I placed her on the bed like the most precious thing in the world.

Because she was.

Unlike her usual pants and tank tops, she wore a lovely floaty dress.

"I don't remember this," I commented idly.

She blushed prettily. "It's, it's new. I was hoping you'd come by."

"I like anything you wear," I sat on the bed next to her. "But this does have some advantages."

Kneeling between her legs I ran my hands up her thighs, under her skirt until I found her panties.

Pulling them off I brushed my fingertip against her slit. She was wet, ready for me.

She was going to have to wait.

"I have to know how you taste," I forced out before I dove upon her and she cried out, her first orgasm almost immediately knocking her out of control.

When finally I had taken my fill she was limp, relaxed upon the bed.

Glowing and beautiful.

"We'll have to do that more often," I teased as I quickly undressed.

"I'm not going to stop you," she said weakly. "I'm not sure I could."

"You could do anything you want with me," I answered as I gently lifted her, drawing the dress off over her head and laying her back down.

She was like a feast before me that I knew I should take my time with, savoring every bite.

But when she wound her arms around my neck again and pulled me close to her, the last few threads that held my restraint frayed.

"Your mine," she whispered softly, her breath hot against my ear as I settled between her legs, the head of my cock pressing against her opening, not yet breaching to the hot, sweet, cave within.

And then she bit my earlobe. And I bucked, sheathing myself inside her in one savage move.

"Now, my mate," she murmured. "Take me now."

And I did.

EPILOGUE: DOTTIE

I walked into the Silver Whale to find Adam was already there. When he saw me, he smiled and waved. I crossed the dining room and sat down at what had become our table in the back corner.

"You don't look happy," he commented.

"I've been dealing with a lot," I gave him a pointed look.

"I don't know what's been going on with me. I swear." He gave me a pleading look. "You believe me, right?"

"You're my brother, Adam. I'm on your side no matter what." I reached across the table to squeeze his hand.

"Thanks, Dottie. I needed to hear that."

We sat in silence until a server came by to take our orders.

"Was there anything else you wanted to talk about?" Adam prompted.

"Yes, actually."

"And here I thought you just wanted to check in on your brother," he teased.

"I wanted to tell you before you found out from someone else," I began.

"Oh, boy." Adam leaned back in his seat. "How bad is it?"

"Jalok and I are together now."

Adam sat forward once more. "That's great, Dottie. You two are well suited for each other."

"Do you mean that?" A smile spread across my face but stopped when Adam started to frown.

"It's what I want to feel," he said after a moment of consideration. "I want to feel happy that you've found someone more than anything. You've been through a lot. You deserve some uncomplicated happiness."

"But?"

"But something inside me is repulsed that you're with him. I hate it."

"I appreciate your honesty." I fought to get the words out. "It's good that you're talking about your feelings."

"They aren't my feelings," Adam groaned. "They're

feelings that I have that I don't want. These feelings don't even feel like mine."

"What do you mean?"

The conversation abruptly stopped when the server arrived with our food.

"Who do you think caught this?" Adam asked.

"Hudd, of course. He brings in the best. The restaurants fight over him every week." I grinned down at the perfect filet of fish on my plate.

"I really missed fish," Adam laughed. "Once trade routes were shut down, Duvest didn't get any fish."

"Dig in."

I gave Adam a few moments to savor his meal before returning to the hard questions.

"Do your feelings not feel like yours?" I prompted.

"No," Adam said in a low voice. "When the Xathi invaded, I hated them with every fiber of my being. The hatred that's inside me now feels nothing like that. It's not mine."

"How is that possible?" I pressed.

"I don't know. I don't even know if I'm right. Something just feels off."

"We don't have to talk about it anymore," I assured him. "Enjoy your lunch."

"That I can do."

I made sure to keep the rest of the conversation

light. When we finished lunch, Adam was in high spirits.

"I'll see you soon, right?" He asked as we walked out of the Silver Whale.

"Of course! Tomorrow, probably."

"Great."

I hugged him extra tightly before we parted ways. I was grateful he didn't ask me where I was going. He wouldn't have liked it.

From the Silver Whale, I walked to Strike Team Three's base camp. Sk'lar arranged for my favorite Valorni pilot to fly me out to the crater at the Vengeance crash site.

I didn't bring any equipment with me this time. It wasn't a work visit but rather a personal one.

"I won't be long," I told my pilot when we landed. "Are you okay with waiting?"

"Sure. A friend of mine is stationed out here. I'll go catch up with him."

"Thanks. I'll come find you."

As I walked across the crater to the tunnel, I noticed the ground moving beneath me. I smiled. On a whim, I touched a random plant growing through the crater floor.

"Can you feel me through this?" I asked.

"*Indeed,*" the Puppet Master replied.

"Interesting. I should've brought my field notes.

That would've made an interesting addition."

"You'll remember. I will agree to let you experiment on that further."

"I'll schedule it."

"You did not bring your tools for collecting data," the Puppet Master observed. *"This leads me to believe you have other motives for coming to see me."*

"Can't I just visit a friend?" I chuckled.

"Of course, but I sense unease within you. Would you care to talk about it?"

"It's my brother. I'm worried about him. I think he's worried too." I traced patterns in the dirt walls with the tip of my finger.

"That tickles," the Puppet Master said.

"You're ticklish?"

"So it would seem."

"Fascinating!"

"Your concerns for your brother are not unfounded," the Puppet Master pressed on. *"I've been keeping watch on him as well."*

"What have you noticed?" A lump of dread formed in the pit of my stomach.

"There are parts of him that do not belong to him," the Puppet Master explained. *"I apologize for not being clearer. That's the only way I know how to describe it. He's quite literally at war with himself."*

"You mean there's something inside him making

him act the way he's been acting?"

"In a sense, yes. It's difficult to describe accurately."

"Will he be all right?" I asked.

"Time will tell."

"I regret introducing you to philosophy," I groaned.

"That's not philosophy. That is a simple fact," the Puppet Master corrected. *"I can't predict the future any better than you can."*

"But you can make an educated guess based on patterns," I contradicted. "Have you seen this before? Is there some kind of pattern to follow?"

"I will look for patterns," the Puppet Master promised. *"While I do that, I request that you take extra precautions in your self-care."*

"Why?"

"You appear to be unaware of what's happening to your body. As your friend, it's my duty to warn you."

"Warn me about what?" Fear tightened in my chest. Was whatever it was inside Adam inside me as well? I couldn't bear it if I started to hate Jalok.

"You must cultivate the life inside of you with care," the Puppet Master advised.

"What?" I blinked in surprise. "Is that your way of telling me to do yoga or meditate?"

"It's my way of telling you that you're growing new life within you."

The world tipped on its axis as the meaning of the

Puppet Master's words settled over me. The Puppet Master's tendrils snaked around my waist and grabbed my arms as I stumbled to the side.

"Are you saying I'm…" I couldn't say it. I didn't want to say it out loud yet. I wanted Jalok to be there the first time I said it out loud.

"Yes. If you need to leave now, I understand."

"Thank you." I wrapped my arms around the thicket's tendril and hugged it. I couldn't be sure, but I thought I heard the Puppet Master laugh.

I ran across the crater to find my Valorni pilot. He flew me back to Kaster as quickly as possible.

Jalok was already in my apartment when I arrived, walking across the living room with a thick sandwich in hand.

"I was just going to lie down," he said quickly.

"I don't believe you," I smirked. The fight with Adam hadn't done much good for his recovering system from the acid attack, but he'd been terrible about following Dr. Parr's bedrest orders.

Her orders weren't unreasonable. Jalok was simply a terrible patient.

"You look happy." His eyes narrowed in suspicion.

"I am," I beamed.

"Did you have a breakthrough in the lab?"

"Nope."

"Did you make a good deal at the market."

"Nope."

"Are you going to keep me guessing?"

"As fun as that would be, nope. I went to see the Puppet Master."

Jalok's eyes widened.

"You know you're not supposed to go on unauthorized trips anymore," he chided. "I have to know where you are in case something happens."

"I'm sorry." I closed the distance between us and put my hand on his arm. "I had lunch with my brother today. It stressed me out. I went to the Puppet Master to ask him to watch Adam."

"And that's what made you happy?"

"No." A smile crept over my expression. Uncontainable joy bubbled up inside me until I thought I was going to burst. "The Puppet Master shared some news with me."

"You've figured out how his lifeforce works?" Jalok guessed.

"Better." I was practically bouncing up and down now.

"What could be better for you than that?"

"I'm pregnant!"

The sandwich Jalok held fell to the floor.

"Are you serious?" He asked.

"The Puppet Master could sense a new life inside of me. Unless I have a tapeworm, I'm pregnant."

"How do you feel about that?" He looked at me like I was an animal ready to spook. I couldn't help but laugh since he was the one who looked like a Luurizi in headlights.

"Freaked out," I admitted. "A little scared. Surprised. Incredibly excited."

"You're excited?" He repeated.

"Of course!" I tossed my head back and laughed. Jalok let out a sigh of relief before scooping me up in his arms and spinning me around.

"Whatever you need, I'm right here for you."

"You," I said between kisses. "I need you."

"I'm here. Always."

PLEASE DON'T FORGET TO LEAVE A REVIEW!

Readers rely on your opinions, and your review can help others decide on what books they read. Make sure your opinion is heard and leave a review where you purchased this book!

Don't miss a new release! You can sign up for release alerts at both Amazon and Bookbub:
bookbub.com/authors/elin-wyn
amazon.com/author/elinwyn

For a free short story, opportunities for advance review copies, release news and the occasional cat picture, please join the newsletter!
https://elinwynbooks.com/newsletter-signup/

And don't forget the Facebook group, where I post sneak peeks of chapters and covers!

https://www.facebook.com/groups/ElinWyn/

LETTER FROM ELIN

Poor Dottie. You know she's going to have her hands full keeping Jalok out of trouble.

Or at least trying.

And he will try, but I suspect that being Jalok, he'll still manage to get into a mess or two.

Next up, more clues into what on earth is going on and another Strike Team member meets his mate in *Tyehn*.

Keep reading for a sneak peak!

XOXO,

Elin

Tyehn

White flakes swirled in the stiff coastal breeze, feeling like gentle fingers massaging my skin.

With a smile on my face, I stood in the Kaster city square next to Jalok as the deluge continued. The snow had covered the stones of the square, making it seem like a solid sheet instead of segmented concrete.

"Isn't this great, Jalok?"

Jalok muttered something incomprehensible and sneezed. He pulled up the collar of his winter coat and huddled within its confines.

Jalok shot me a dirty look, snow forming on his scalp.

"No, it's not great. Leave it to a Valorni to think this inhospitable weather is somehow a positive."

"Bah, come on. Don't you just love the way it blankets everything with a pristine coat? Like we're on a planet untouched by sapient incursion."

Our voices had a muted edge due to the snow absorbing sound.

I found the crisp, fresh snow to be bracing and invigorating. It made everything new, like it was a world that could have a fresh start.

Void knew, Ankou could use one.

My companion, apparently, didn't enjoy it as much.

"It's cold, it's wet, and I think I'm coming down with something, so why don't you just can the relentless cheer and let me suffer in silence?"

I chuckled at his griping.

"Come on, Jalok, doesn't your girlfriend live in this city?"

"What's that got to do with anything, you overgrown oaf?"

"You should think about how much fun you're going to have once you're off duty rather than complaining about the snow, that's all I'm saying"

His expression softened about one iota, but I figured that the best I was going to get out of the grumpy Skotan.

We stood outside of the government building on the

edge of the public square, having finished our recon and awaiting further instructions from our team leader Sk'lar. It was kind of boring, to be honest, but the snow was a wonderful distraction.

"Jalok, did you know that every inch of snow equals ten inches of rain?"

"No, and I don't give a srell."

"Well, you should. Think about it."

"I don't want to. I just want to get out of this damn cold. The Skotan home world isn't plagued by this revolting phenomenon you seem so enchanted by."

"If this were rain and not snow, we'd have had twenty inches by now. The square would be flooded, and it would be even worse."

"That is a matter of opinion."

We were not just in Kaster because Jalok's girlfriend lived there. The anti-alien movement had been building momentum in this area, and Strike Team Three had been reassigned here.

The blanket of fresh snow disguised numerous stains—some of them from blood—on the square due to the recent riots.

It was hard not to take it personally when a growing contingent humans were out protesting our rights to exist.

They had the right to free speech, of course.

And honestly, I never expected everyone to always get along.

But the more radicalized elements of their movement had taken to acts of sabotage and terrorism, attacking humans as well as aliens.

We could take it, but the humans were more fragile.

Things had been peaceful for a short while, but we all knew that it could boil over again at any time.

Which is why we'd been dispatched here. Without the use of the rifts, we couldn't always deploy rapidly enough to prevent more violence.

Finally, our comm units crackled, picking up static from the storm, and Sk'lar's curt voice came over the line.

"Jalok and Tyehn, report."

"Just finished a circuit of the square, Commander." I smiled down at Jalok. "Now we're enjoying the weather."

Jalok flipped me the bird, a gesture he picked up from the humans, and I chuckled anew. Apparently the middle finger represents a human phallic symbol.

Human men must be tiny.

"Did you see anything amiss?"

"Negative, Commander. The snow is keeping the anti-alienists inside today, it seems."

"They're smarter than us." Jalok was smart enough to keep his grumbling off comms.

Sk'lar was a real ball buster, and getting laid hasn't mellowed him out as much as we'd hoped.

"I see. It doesn't hurt to be cautious, however. You two should make another circuit of the square, and then head over to Cazak and Navat's position."

"Copy that. Tyehn out."

"Damn it, he wants us to do more walking in this frozen rain?"

"Actually, Jalok, despite common belief, snow is not, in fact, frozen rain. That's a different atmospheric phenomenon. Rather, the water in the atmosphere condenses directly—"

"For fuck's sake, shut up. We're not all hydrologists, you know. All I want is a warm heating unit and a cold brew, not to have a science lesson."

"Suit yourself."

I didn't take Jalok's complaints personally.

Everyone knows he's got an attitude. The less generous would say he's a pain in the ass—another human expression, and this time it made sense.

We walked back out from under the awning under which we'd stood—not that it kept the snow off much anyway, or at least not enough to keep Jalok from complaining.

Our footprints were already half filled before we'd made it a hundred yards. I glanced behind us, seeing a large set and a smaller set trailing behind us.

Nothing else. No one was out in this weather, at least not marching around.

"I wish the anti-alienists were up to no good today. A good fight might actually warm me up some." Jalok muttered. "Dottie wouldn't have to find out."

I decided to be a bit sympathetic. Jalok wasn't really a man who'd expected to find his mate on an alien world, if ever.

Learning that she didn't exactly approve of his more violent tendencies had been a bit of a shock. He'd done well, toning things down, but it had taken a toll on his already rough temper.

"Why don't we swing by the main avenue after our next sweep? There's a coffee stand there. We can warm up for a bit and take it to go."

"Finally, you say something that doesn't piss me off. Good thinking, for a Valorni."

I glanced at him askance. "Aren't you a little bit troubled by the irony of making racist remarks while we're on patrol for people who are, in fact, racist?"

"More like species-ist, but I get your point. I just don't give a srell."

We grew silent, trudging on through the snow for a time with only our muted footfalls and his occasional sneezes to keep us company.

A human woman glared out of a second story apartment at us, her gaze full of suspicion. I smiled and waved at her cheerfully. Her sneer grew by a mile before she jerked her curtains shut.

"Why do you keep trying?"

"Diplomacy is the first recourse, remember? Then de-escalation, and then, finally, if there's no other alternative, reasonable force."

"I don't need a reason to use force. Force is its own reason."

I couldn't help but laugh at his gung ho attitude.

Skotan are known to be hot tempered, but Jalok was like a Skotan with a little extra Skotan added in.

We reached the café I'd mentioned, cheerfully lit, warm and inviting. We headed inside and were enveloped by the heat coming from an overhead vent. Jalok paused directly underneath, opening his collar to let the warm air flow into his uniform.

"Hello." I smiled huge at the human attendant.

Her gaze was as cold as the snow, maybe even colder. I could tell she was considering giving us a hard time for being 'aliens' but I pulled my lapel back on the coat to reveal the insignia of Strike Team Three.

That made a huge difference in her service, if not her attitude. Sure, every alien she'd ever seen was part of the military, one way or another.

But it was one thing to give a hard time to someone who was passing through.

Something else entirely when it was someone

stationed here, working with the local guards.

I ordered two coffees.

I couldn't resist taking a sip right away at the counter, and then carried our cups to the high pub table Jalok had chosen.

He sneered at me and shook his head as I deposited his drink in front of him.

"What's wrong? I thought you liked this bitter swill."

"The problem's not the drink." He pointed at my face. "It's the whipped cream on your big honking nose. You look ridiculous."

"Oh." I chuckled as I used my tongue to lick the dollop of cream off my nose. "Did I get it?"

"Ugh, yes, you disgusting freak. Next time use a napkin."

I shrugged and sat down across from him. Technically we were on duty, but a with the snow blanketing the city Kaster is dead as can be. I figured a few minutes sipping drinks to warm both Jalok's body and his attitude wouldn't be too gross a dereliction.

"So, how are things going with Dottie?"

Jalok almost smiled—almost.

"Good." He drank from his cup, not bothering to blow on it cool the liquid.

"Good? That's all I'm getting out of you?"

"Well, I'm not going to describe our sex life, if that's what you were wondering."

It wasn't what I had been wondering about, but quite frankly I was a bit curious as to what it would be like to sleep with a human woman.

So many of our crew had found their mates, but I still hadn't seen the attraction.

They were interesting...but nothing had ever sparked inside me when I'd seen one.

"I don't expect you to give me intimate details, just... what's it like? Being with a human, I mean. Does she get freaked out by your scales?"

"No." He took a drink of his coffee and sighed. "Now this is good."

"I heard Dottie didn't like you at first."

Jalok glared at me over his steaming cup.

"Who the hell told you that?"

"I don't remember, probably Cazak."

"Figures."

"They said that when you went berserk during the riots and put all those people in the hospital she was a little spooked, but then you guys became friends."

"Look, you go ahead and believe what you want. Doesn't matter to me a lick. Now finish your drink before Sk'lar starts complaining—oh, speak of the devil."

Our comms lit up, and sure enough Sk'lar demanded to know why we hadn't returned to our assigned position.

I drained the remains of my drink in one big gulp and hastily followed Jalok back into the snow.

Maki

I gave my ropes three sharp tugs and pulled at the clasps of my harness. One of the clasps was a little rusty so I switched it out for a new one.

I went through harness clasps like those alien soldiers went through blaster ammo.

I checked the strength of the branch my ropes were tied to. Sturdy, healthy and perfect for ziplining.

Last month, I spent my whole day off trekking through the forest putting up the perfect ziplining course. It wasn't every day that I could do something like that.

I had to wait until all of the forest creatures were either in hibernation or at least out of nesting season.

Nothing like overprotective mamas with four hundred teeth to ruin one's hike.

The living vines were a whole other story.

Some of them belong to the Puppet Master who, by all means, is a real pal. The others belonged to an array of species that liked to wrap around my ankles and attempt to drag me underground.

Figuring out which was which was always good fun.

I tentatively touched the weapon at my side.

It was of my own invention, specially designed to handle those pesky living vines that were friends rather than foes.

Unfortunately, those nasty vines looked just like the Puppet Master's friendly tendrils. At least once, I've stabbed the needle-thin barred blade of my weapon into the flesh of the Puppet Master.

I'd never spoken to the Puppet Master but I'd heard from some of my coworkers that if someone touches the Puppet Master, it can hear their thoughts.

Since my mother raised me right, the moment I realized I stabbed the wrong vine, I pressed my hand into the Puppet Master and apologized profusely.

I swore I heard it laugh.

Ever since that day, I felt safer going on my solo excursions in the forest.

It was like I had a spotter without having to deal with the company of people who didn't know what they were doing.

Maybe it wasn't the brightest plan, depending on a giant plant-creature I'd never seen, but it made sense in my head.

My coworkers thought I was insane for doing this sort of stuff on my day off. Most of them liked to sit in dark pubs or take shuttles to the bigger cities on their days off.

That sounded boring to me but I didn't judge them for it.

Except… shopping. Really?

It wasn't my fault that I was born with a high adventure drive.

I entirely blamed my father, and thanked him as well.

He had a lust for adventure too. I learned everything I knew about handling myself in the wilderness from him.

Nearly every weekend of my childhood was spent camping, climbing, and jumping off things no rational person would ever jump off.

My happiest memories were spent in the basement where my mother worked in her at-home lab.

Best childhood ever.

I tipped my face to the sunlight and let it warm my

skin. A gentle breeze picked up. Without opening my eyes, I stepped off the branch.

My weight settled quickly and comfortably into my harness as I zipped through the trees. Birds and other small forest creatures darted out of my way as I came as close to flying as I'd ever get.

I landed on the platform at the end of the zip line.

One click to unclasp myself and another to attach me to the next line and I was on my way. I'd gotten the zip line transfer movements down to a science.

One of the questions I was often asked was why do I put hours of effort into a zip line excursion that ultimately lasts less than ten minutes.

What people didn't understand is that the trek all the way out here, the preparation, and the double-checking were all part of the fun.

The final ride was almost a bonus, seeing how all your planning worked out.

The forest started to thin out as I zipped down the last leg of my self-made course. My bike waited where I parked it at the base of the final tree. As I flew through the canopy, I loosed a sigh of relief.

On more than one occasion, I'd finished a hike or a zip line course to find that my bike had been moved somewhere.

Probably the work of any number of forest dwellers. Either that or a disturbingly dedicated prankster.

With adrenaline coursing through my veins, I unhooked my harness and practically slid down the tree trunk.

And that's where my perfect day hit its first bump.

A blinking red light on my comm unit.

My stomach tightened for a moment. A message from home?

I hit play, and gnawed at my lip, only relaxing when my boss's voice filled the forest air. "Maki, I know it's your day off, but I need you to stop by." Dr. Illiux Band laughed. "You'll find it interesting."

Ooh.

I'd finished my last assignment a few days ago, and had been anxious to see what was next.

It might be fair to say I had a low boredom threshold.

Maybe.

A friend of mine helped me rig up my bike a few years back. Instead of an ignition, all my sweet baby needed was a handprint scan. It would only start for me.

If I wanted to, I could calibrate someone else's handprint into the bikes memory stores so that they could start my bike.

It went without saying that I never wanted to do that.

There was a greater chance of me zip lining

between the stars without a helmet than letting someone else ride my bike.

I placed my handprint on the scanner between the handlebars.

My buddy also installed a small console so I could get in touch with people should I get in an accident, use my navigational tracker in unfamiliar territory, and participate in conference calls while I'm en route to a job site.

The handprint scanner flared green as my bike started up. The tire rims lit up bright blue. Blue streaks of light ignited over the black frame. The engine was blessedly quiet. The best thing my father ever taught me was how to listen to nature. As much as I loved my bike, I didn't like that it disrupted the natural sounds around me so I had that remedied.

Now, my bike was the perfect vehicle. It was jungle friendly, desert friendly and city friendly which was perfect since I spent an equal amount of time in all three settings. Mountains? No problem.

Rocky terrain? Easy as Qigla pie.

My stomach rumbled.

Wow, I could go for a Qigla pie right about now. I already ate through the nutrient bars I packed this morning.

No matter how many times I'd done this, I've never

correctly anticipated how many nutrient bars it takes to fill me up.

As I rumbled through the jungle on my bike, I spied an unusually dense looking patch of earth. I gently slowed by bike and hopped off. I picked up a pinch of dirt and rolled it between my fingers. It had an odd texture. I couldn't say I'd ever left something similar. It hadn't eaten away at my skin so that was a good sign.

The earth around Sauma was amazing. There were soil concentrations only found in this area. That's why I moved here to work.

I pulled a sample vial out of my pack and scooped up some of the dirt. This would be fun to analyze later.

I didn't like sitting still for extended periods of time.

When I first moved to Sauma, I loved being in the lab day in and day out. I got that from my mother.

After a month or so, I started getting restless. Luckily, there were a number of clubs in Sauma.

I was in a club for other bikers. We rode together once a week though sometimes I met up with a handful of people just for quick rides.

I was also part of a free-running group. We specialized in leaping through abandoned buildings.

Actually, it was through a member of the free-running group that I discovered an archaeology team that occasionally sourced locals from Sauma to work on their digs.

As someone who was interested in archaeology but not fully trained, I signed up the first chance I got.

Digs didn't happen very often, but I relished them all the same, even if it was just for grunt work.

Forest gave way to outpost shacks and farms then eventually to city streets. I wove through pedestrians with ease until I reached my building.

My boss, Dr. Illiux Band, was waiting for me when I walked in the door.

"Sorry for calling you in on your day off but it couldn't wait," he grinned. "Here's your next assignment." He passed me a datapad. "We have a team on a new project and you know the rules - they're going to need an independent observer to help and make sure everything is right and proper. "

I opened up the tab with the location information first and imported it into my bike's console.

"You're going to the Sika Jungle. It's not far. You should be able to get there in less than an hour on that bike of yours."

I analyzed the map that popped up on my console. Five trails to the site appeared on the console, four of which I was already familiar with.

"I'll head out now," I told my boss. "There's an unexplored trail that's calling my name."

"Don't get yourself killed before you get there," he warned me.

"I would never dream of being that rude."

Tyehn

Jalok and I trudged up the ramp leading inside our shuttle craft.

The rest of team three was already on board as our eyes adjusted to the relative gloom. After being outside in the blazing white of a snowstorm, the shuttle's cabin seemed darker than a cave.

I bumped Navat's closed fist by way of greeting as I

settled in to the seat next to him. As the only other Valorni on Team Three, we took care of each other.

It's weird, because had it not been for the stranding I doubt we would have been friends. Before we joined the crew of the *Vengeance*, I'd been a scientist, and he was a laborer, so other than being of the same species we don't have a lot in common.

Then the Xathi came, and we all had to become soldiers.

Even now that the bugs seem a past threat, we continued on in our new roles, only now our enemies were food shortages and political unrest.

The more things changed, the more they stayed the same, or so the humans said.

"For fuck's sake, close the damn ramp." Jalok shivered, and added a sneeze for emphasis.

"Not yet." Sk'lar peered out the back of the shuttle. "We have one more passenger."

"What? But the squad's all here."

Jalok craned his neck about, searching the cabin for the rest of our team.

"I see Cazak's ugly ass, and the two big cows, and a beady eyed K'ver, and I know I'm sitting here on account of the fact that I'm freezing to death. Who the hell else is left? Did we get a new recruit?"

Sk'lar grins wryly at Jalok.

"We're taking a scientist with us as well who needs a lift to the capital. Bide."

"I don't want to bide. When the scientist gets here, I'm going to kick his ass for making me cold." He scowled. "I've got two weeks of furlough coming, and want to get something nice for Dottie."

Light footfalls barely made an echo on the ramp, announcing a new passenger coming onboard. When I saw who it was, I had to stifle a laugh.

Cazak noticed too, and shot his cousin Jalok a wry grin.

"What was that you were saying about our passenger?" Cazak's tone dripped with nonchalant innocence. Jalok noticed it, but being Jalok he didn't stop to ponder the significance of it.

"I said, I'm gonna kick their ass."

The scientist stood behind Jalok's chair, arms crossed over her chest. She glanced around the cabin, took in our stifled smiles, and got herself up to speed really quick.

"Just like you did to those rioters a while back, right?"

Like a good little fish, Jalok rose to the bait.

"No, not just like the rioters. What I do to this human is going to make me seem like a pacifist. I'll break his arms, his legs, and then knock all his teeth out for good measure."

"You're going to knock my teeth out?"

Jalok's eyes went wide when he heard Dottie's voice. He leaped to his feet and turned around, face a mask of incredulity.

"Dottie? You're the scientist?"

"Oh, don't let me stop you, babe, you're on a roll." She raised an eyebrow and glared. Jalok squirmed under her disapproving gaze.

"I—that is, I didn't know it would be—you look pretty today, babe."

The rest of Team Three—even Sk'lar, let out an *aww* in unison as if to say, how cute.

Jalok gritted his teeth and tried to keep a smile on his face, even though we all knew he was fuming.

"Thanks." Dottie got on her tip toes and kissed Jalok on the cheek. His tension and anger seemed to drain away.

"Ah, I'm sure you know everyone here, right Dottie?"

I marveled at the way that Jalok's whole demeanor changed with Dottie present. It was almost like he wasn't an insufferable srell.

Almost.

"You know Cazak's ugly ass, of course, but the big bald guy with purple stripes on his shoulders is Tyehn. You two should get along great, given he's a scientist."

"Charmed." I offered my hand for a shake, as was the

human custom. Her hand was swallowed by my much larger mitt.

"Likewise."

"The other big, bald guy is Navat."

"Pleased to meet you."

"And you as well."

"We're glad you're here, Dottie."

Dottie turned to Cazak and arched an eyebrow.

"Why is that?"

"Because Jalok is so much less of a dick when you're around."

"Aww, thanks guys." Dottie smiled sweetly at Cazak. Jalok tried to pretend he wasn't furious with his cousin with limited success.

The ramp finally closed up. Jalok and Dottie took up seats near the rear of the shuttle while the rest of us politely pretended they were not present.

"So what are you going to do with your furlough, Tyehn?"

I glanced over at Cazak and shrugged.

"I'm not sure. I'd like to hang out with some of the new friends I've made, both human and otherwise. You?"

"I'm going to try and find a nice hole in the wall and drink myself into oblivion, like I do every furlough."

As if in answer to our planning, Sk'lar headed up to the cockpit as an emergency comm came through.

He listened to it grimly, spoke quietly to the person on the other end, and returned minutes later, his lips a thin, tight line.

"Bad news, Team Three."

"Isn't it always?"

Sk'lar ignored Cazak's comment.

"It looks like our furlough's been canceled."

"What? No way." Jalok seemed particularly disgruntled, even for him. I guess he was planning on spending some quality time with Dottie.

"So, we're not going to Nyheim?" I asked.

"We're going to Nyheim, but the team will remain on call. That means no getting piss drunk in case we get called out on a mission."

"What happened?"

Sk'lar turns to Navat grimly.

"There's been some 'civil unrest' at one of the smaller colonies up the coast. Security forces have it handled—for now—but we're going to remain on alert in case they need back up."

All of Team Three displayed their dismay as per their own way. Jalok complained, Navat sighed heavily, Cazak shook his head, and I merely shrugged. I was disappointed as much as the others, but I didn't see a point it getting all worked up over it.

We spent most of the ride to Nyheim in silence, all lost in our own thoughts. The exceptions were Dottie and Jalok, who continued to converse in low tones at the rear of the shuttle.

Our craft lurched to a stop, the landing pylons came down, and soon we were all tramping down the ramp.

"Remember, we're on call." Sk'lar glared at Cazak in particular. "You'd better be fit for duty when and if the call comes in."

"Yes sir."

Cazak gave a sarcastic salute that became an obscene gesture when Sk'lar turned his back to converse with our pilot.

"Who's hungry?"

Cazak and Navat turned to face me, as Dottie and Jalok strode off through the snow, hand in hand.

Part of me envied what they had, but I'd never be attracted to a human woman.

"Are you buying?"

"Not likely. I thought we'd go hit that ramen place Sylor took us to last time we were here."

"Sounds good to me."

"Me, too."

The three of us traipsed through the snowfall into Nyheim's busy downtown area. Most folks were friendly, especially the merchants—everyone knew soldiers had credits to spare when off duty—but some of the humans gave us baleful glares.

It seemed like the anti-alien sentiment had spread all over the colonies.

We did our best to ignore the glares and made our way to the ramen place. Navat pushed the door open, and we were greeted by a warm blast of air and the inviting smell of noodles and soup.

My belly rumbled like thunder as we strode up to the counter and made our orders.

Soon we were ensconced at a booth near the corner of the room, so we could watch all around us. With all of the anti-alien sentiment going around, we figured it couldn't hurt to be cautious.

As the three of us chowed down on our dinner, I couldn't help but overhear snippets of the myriad conversations going on around the diner. A lot of folks were talking—or more aptly, complaining—about the snowfall, which made sense.

There were more than a few people worried about food shortages. Supposedly, that situation was pretty much handled, but it didn't mean that people weren't still worried about it.

A few others talked about whether or not we could really trust the Puppet Master, but it was the pair at the booth next to us that was of particular interest.

One was a Valorni like myself and Navat, and he had his left arm in a sling. His human companion seemed to be inquiring about the injury.

"Does it hurt much?"

"Not anymore. The medics said I'd be able to lose the sling tomorrow, but it's a precaution."

"And you say Marin just flipped out on you? Out of nowhere."

"Yeah. One minute we were joking about how General Rouhr gets that line between his eyes when he's angry, the next he's going off on my about how I'm alien scum and I need to get off 'his' planet."

"The fuck, man?"

"I know. Then he grabbed a coil spanner and stabbed me in the arm with it."

"Wow. Did he get arrested?"

"You think? Of course he did. But I was talking to the guards, and it seems like he's not the only guy to just sort of lose it lately. From zero to full on xenophobe in a second flat."

The three of us at our table exchanged glances. We'd all heard of someone who'd had a sudden, drastic change in attitude. Brass said it was being looked into, but that didn't reassure us.

Not in the least.

Get Tyehn Now!

https://elinwynbooks.com/conquered-world-alien-romance/

DON'T MISS THE STAR BREED!

Given: Star Breed Book One

When a renegade thief and a genetically enhanced mercenary collide, space gets a whole lot hotter!

Thief Kara Shimsi has learned three lessons well - keep her head down, her fingers light, and her tithes to the syndicate paid on time.

But now a failed heist has earned her a death sentence - a one-way ticket to the toxic Waste outside the dome. Her only chance is a deal with the syndicate's most ruthless enforcer, a wolfish mountain of genetically-modified muscle named Davien.

The thought makes her body tingle with dread-or is it heat?

Mercenary Davien has one focus: do whatever is necessary to get the credits to get off this backwater mining colony and back into space. The last thing he wants is a smart-mouthed thief - even if she does have the clue he needs to hunt down whoever attacked the floating lab he and his created brothers called home.

Caring is a liability. Desire is a commodity. And love could get you killed.

https://elinwynbooks.com/star-breed/

ABOUT THE AUTHOR

I love old movies – *To Catch a Thief, Notorious, All About Eve* — and anything with Katherine Hepburn in it. Clever, elegant people doing clever, elegant things.

I'm a hopeless romantic.

And I love science fiction and the promise of space.

So it makes perfect sense to me to try to merge all of those loves into a new science fiction world, where dashing heroes and lovely ladies have adventures, get into trouble, and find their true love in the stars!